I0592668

COPYRIGHT

National Library of Australia Cataloguing-in-Publication data:

Sarah's Story / Danielle Aitken

Editors: Helen Batziris / Phillip Aitken

Cover: Karen Mc Dermott / Danielle Aitken

Interior design: Vellum

ISBN: 978-0-6484000-9-7(sc) ISBN: 978-0-6484000-8-0(e)

SARAH'S STORY LIFE AFTER IVF

A Story Of Personal Triumph And Spiritual Growth.

DANIELLE AITKEN

DEDICATION

This book is dedicated to Kerry and all of the amazing women and men I have met along the way, who have bravely embarked upon the IVF journey.

I also dedicate this book to all the brilliant doctors, embryologists, nurses and scientists who make it possible for so many to achieve their goal to be parents.

ACKNOWLEDGMENTS

I would like to thank my beautiful family, friends and colleagues for being with me on this journey and for the valuable lessons of a lifetime.

Eternal gratitude to Phil, who has carried me when I could not carry myself.

Special thanks to Helen Batziris for her expertise in editing. I am forever grateful.

Shalom

Author Danielle Aitken knows how to craft a real tear-jerker of a story, taking readers deep into the process of conception when biology is against you. It's clear that Aitken knows a great deal about the IVF process, and that expertise is put into heavy detail to really show readers the difficulties that Sarah and Matt experience in order to have something which comes so naturally to so many others.

The prose is well written and gives a strong sense of what's going on in Sarah's head, and the profound realisations which she comes to in the latter half of the book really turn the narrative in an unexpectedly beautiful way.....

Sarah's Story: A Story of Personal Triumph and Spiritual Growth gives a true account of the dramas of life, but also gives hope for the strength and resilience of the human spirit against adversity.

5 STAR Review by K.C. Finn

Readers' Favorite international book reviews.

* * *

Just finished reading Sarah's Story.

This debut novel by author Danielle Aitken, shares the emotional journey of one woman and her husband as they struggle with infertility as they try to start a family.

It gives enormous insight to the various aspects of IVF and the inner pressure that comes with trying to conceive. It tugs at the heart-strings in the early chapters but then soars into showing true resilience. It also is ultimately a story about love and how a strong relationship and the mindset to keep pushing forward can overcome life's setbacks. Great read.

5 STAR Review by Kelly Van Nelson.

Poet and Amazon bestselling Author of Graffiti Lane.

* * *

Danielle has created such a moving tale, that is more than just a story about IVF. It's a story woven to capture that beating, human heart, it's about survival and being brave. It's about getting back up and on with things again, once you've allowed those tears to fall.

It's a story about allowing yourself to be human, to reflect and acknowledge the pain, the past, the why? To be able to move forward Into the future with the answer to our 'why' becoming clearer.

When we all remember our 'Why'?, it makes life all the more greater!

Congratulations on a moving story Danielle, I can't wait to see what you come out with next!

"Move over Jodi Picoult, Danielle Aitken is on the rise."

5 STAR Review by Michelle Weitering.

Author of Thirteen and Underwater.

SARAH'S STORY LIFE
AFTER IVF

CONTENTS

PART I
MY INNOCENCE

CHAPTER 1
IN THE BEGINNING

My name is Sarah, and this is my story.

It was mid-1960 when I made my way into this world. I was a mistake I believe, although Mum would never put it quite like that. Birth control back then pretty much consisted of less sophisticated methods such as; condoms, withdrawal or even complete abstinence, a choice adopted by many women trying to avoid *yet* another baby.

My mother, good Catholic that she is, adopted the rhythm method, lovingly nicknamed by some '*the rhythm method of conception*', not *contraception*, and thank goodness for that, because the end result eight and a half months later was me.

This happy event came about four years after the last of my three older siblings Rick was born. Peter was the second eldest, and Melissa, my eldest sibling was then eight and a half years old.

Melissa, from all accounts, was not impressed to have a screaming baby in the house because peace in the previously "perfectly spaced family" was forever shattered by the arrival of a colicky baby - me. I announced my arrival by creating a huge disruption, the likes of which can only be caused by a newborn baby, and no one was spared.

Mum was not to be deterred by this small unplanned hiccup however, and so believing that I needed a playmate closer to my own age, set about providing me with one. Dad, of course, also had a little to do with this. The only thing they didn't count on was the line of fraternal twins on Mum's side of the family. Her grandmother was a non-identical twin, and thus four was soon to become six and Dad, even sooner than that, had an appointment made and was scheduled to attend Doc Wilson's clinic for a *'voluntary'* vasectomy.

His feet hardly touched the ground. I believe Mum's exact words were, 'Doc Wilson is expecting you at nine on Tuesday, it's either that or you can move permanently in with Stinky.' Stinky was our much loved, although slightly odorous, Golden Retriever. Now, although Stinky's kennel was the envy of all the neighbourhood dogs, and quite a tempting offer, Dad reluctantly chose Doc Wilson.

Yes, I grew up in quite a large family; two sisters, three brothers, eleven cousins and plenty of aunts and uncles to ensure that there was never a dull moment. There was always plenty of family, and plenty of food. No one ever left without having a meal and our door was always open. Children were a part of daily life, which was great for my siblings and for me, because there was never a shortage of someone to play with.

Family and friends dropped in any time, day or night, and they knew they were always welcome. To me, it seemed a little like a party most of the time.

I had a very happy childhood. I loved my parents and they were wonderful role models. Mum worked as a nurse at the local hospital three days a week on the children's ward. It was obvious to everyone who met her that she had an extremely loving and generous nature. As kids we never doubted her love. We knew that she would always be there for us; anytime, anywhere.

Whenever any of my older brothers got themselves into trouble at school, Mum was always there. When Ricky Stevenson from next door, fell off the backyard trampoline and broke his arm in three places, Mum was there. His own mum fainted after taking one brief look at the unfortunate angle of Ricky's forearm, but *my* mum was unfazed and dealt with mother and son with ease and expertise.

That was just what Mum did, she cared for all. When the girl up the road got herself pregnant, which we were not supposed to know about, Mum was there, even when the girl's own parents were not. All the kids in the neighbourhood knew that Mrs Johnston could always be depended on in times of crisis. There was also an understanding that she could be discreet when required. This of course did not guarantee that she would not go straight to the offender's parents if she felt it was appropriate, but even this did not alter the fact that generally Mum was respected by all.

As I grew up, I do recall those times when I thought Mum was a bit too compassionate for her own good, and for the work she was doing on the children's ward. There were days when she would come home from work red faced, with tears in her eyes. We all knew that she had been crying. On these days, she would sit in the backyard with Dad, to debrief I suppose. We knew that these were the times we had to make ourselves scarce. Dad would often give us thirty cents each to go and buy an icy pole from the local store. 'Eat it at the park', he would tell us 'Take your time.'

Things were different then. We were safe to roam the streets until dark. These were the days when we knew something bad had happened at Mum's work. She would tell us that sometimes the children were very sick and sometimes there was nothing that could be done for them but make them comfortable and pray.

I'm sure she loved them all to some degree, but there were the special ones: the long stayers. These were the children that really got to Mum. I think she felt like they were part of her big extended family. Perhaps she shouldn't have got so close at times but she couldn't help it, it was just the way she was, and I don't think that she would have wanted it any other way. Mum used to say to Dad, 'the day I stop caring will be the day I hand in my resignation.' Her favourite quote was: '*Through pain we grow, if it doesn't kill you, it makes you stronger.*' This was how she lived life and viewed work. Her days of pain and sadness seemed to make her stronger and even more determined to go back the next day.

These were special kids, and Mum would remind us of this whenever we complained of the trivial aliments to try to get a day off school. She would say, 'they haven't been blessed with good health like all of you kids, but they soldier on and face whatever the day dishes out to them, and you will too'. We could never have a 'sickie'. Don't get me wrong, she was compassionate and caring to us when we *were* sick, but she had a radar that you could never fool. I don't remember her ever being wrong. She knew when we were sick, even before we knew ourselves.

Then there was Dad, a strong affectionate man, who loved his wife more than life itself, and loved us just as much. He was bigger than the average dad. A hug from Dad was quite an experience. If he gave you a bear hug, he would lift you off your feet and take your breath away. 'Dad, I can't breathe put me down', never got the response intended. He would just squeeze more and smother you in kisses. The more you protested, the longer the ordeal lasted. Most often, I didn't mind though. It was actually nice, except of course when it was done in front of a boy you were trying to impress. '*DAD! NOT COOL!*', but that never stopped him.

Have you ever heard that old playground taunt that kids used to say to each other in the schoolyard? You know, in the most threatening voice you could muster '*my dad is bigger than your dad!*', yes, I know it's very corny, but seriously, it was true. All the kids knew it. This fact alone allowed me a certain amount of respect in the play-ground, that many of the less fortunate kids with, shall we say, '*less intimidating fathers*', did not get. I was not opposed to using this advantage whenever I needed. His arms were the talk of all the neighbourhood boys. He had great fun flexing his biceps and letting my brothers and their friends hang off his flexed muscles. Oh, and there was of course the ongoing and fairly futile '*Competition of Champions*' a.k.a. *arm wrestling with Mr Johnston.* This competi-tion comprised of, as you may expect, my dad challenging anyone who was game, left or right arm, it didn't matter. No one ever beat him that I can remember. As a child I just thought that all dads were like my dad; big, full of silly jokes and sporting a really embar-rassing sense of humour. Of course, I now know this is most defi-nitely not the case, and probably a good thing too, although I would never tell Dad that.

Dad's muscles were possibly the result of good genes and definitely the result of working long and hard as a labourer on building sites. Back in those days, men were men and Occupational Health and Safety rules did not apply. Lift it or be considered a *girl,* which was the ultimate insult, by those who would lift it if you didn't.

Fast forward thirty years, and Dad's back is pretty well *stuffed,* but you will never ever hear stoic Dad complain about it. '*Real men don't complain*' according to Dad. Mum scoffs at this stupidity, and insists he takes his pain killers and anti-inflammatories when she thinks it is troubling him, and he is wise enough to do as he is told. '*Happy wife, happy life*', has always been Dad's motto, but just quietly, I think he is relieved when Mum reads him the riot act. He actually gets to have some well-deserved relief, without ever having to admit he really needed it in the first place.

All in all, it was comforting growing up with Dad in the house. We always felt safe and even though we had our family tussles and disagreements we always knew that he was dependable—however, it was *never* a good move to deliberately disobey him—his word was law in our house. Well, actually, Mum's word was law, because in the pecking order, she sat right at the top. That aside, Dad did have a temper and although we didn't see it very often, we all knew, if you crossed him, or worse than that, if you upset Mum, you could guarantee you would be in *huge* trouble.

A lot of my time as a young girl was spent helping Mum with the twins, Karen and Billy. Although, I was only two years older than them, it was clear from a very early stage that my maternal instinct was alive and well. At the tender age of five, I used to push them in the pram, no easy feat for a five-year-old. I also watched them for Mum when she had a shower, or so she let me think. Years later, she told me that she could see us all the whole time through the ajar bathroom door, via the reflection in the bathroom mirror. Although at the time my pride was somewhat wounded by this revelation, upon reflection I'm not so sure I would leave three-year-old twins in the care of a five-year-old for very long unobserved either.

The upside of this slight deception was that I actually thought I had been given a precious *grown up* responsibility. I was in charge, which was an enormous self-esteem booster and for me this somehow seemed to reinforce the fact that one day I knew I would be a mother too, and what's more, I would be good at it.

I'm not exactly sure when it was I realised I wanted to be a mother. I don't think it was ever a conscious choice. I knew it when I was looking after the twins, and I have known it every day since. I fully expected that I would have a house filled with an adoring husband, plenty of children, family and friends, exactly like the home I had grown up in.

When I reflect back on this time, I find it interesting to note that my elder sister Melissa, who at that stage was thirteen years old, wanted nothing to do with the sharing of such family responsibilities. This was not something that I was aware of at the time but looking back it seemed very obvious.

The older boys Peter and Rick appeared to stay clear too. They were happy to just do boy *stuff* together. They chose to fly below the radar, and therefore managed to avoid a lot of the extra duties that got dished out if you were lurking about with nothing to do.

Melissa seemed to be left out on her own by the developing family dynamics. The boys had each other, and I had the twins, but this was something she didn't seem to mind too much. In fact, she appeared to revel in it. With every passing month she seemed to be getting more and more erratic and grumpy. I didn't understand it and I'm not sure she did either, but it was as though she didn't want anything to do with any of us. For her, and for the rest of the family, it was not to be an easy transition through the teenage years. By the time Melissa was seventeen years old, she hated us all at different times, although never all at once. She always made sure she had some allies to close ranks with when she was directing her tirade towards one of the others. Mostly though, she would set her sights on Mum and let rip.

Mum took a lot of abuse from Melissa over the years, but despite everything, Mum never stopped loving her. As a young girl, I heard things that I should never have heard. I heard my precious mother being verbally abused in the most horrible of ways. I heard Melissa swear at Mum often and always with such aggression and hatred. She used words that I knew were the worst kind of swear words. I heard her say unspeakable things to our mother. For some reason it seemed she really wanted to hurt Mum. I didn't understand it at the time. All I know is that it was a horrible time in the household, because you never knew when a tirade was coming. One minute everything was peaceful and the next, for no apparent reason other than perhaps Melissa had not got her own way, world war three would break out. There would be screaming and door slamming, and then quiet again. To the outside world, Mum seemed to take it all in her stride, but more than once I caught her crying in her bathroom when she thought no one was around. She tried to pretend that it didn't hurt her, but it did.

When I was nine years old, in a juvenile attempt to make Mum feel better, I remember saying to her 'we don't love Melissa anymore, do we?'

Mum spun around so quickly, and without the slightest hesitation said, 'Of course we love Melissa, Sarah, why would you say such a thing?'

'You don't love her as much as you love the rest of us though, because she is so mean to you.' I stated, as a matter of fact.

To me this was as obvious as adding two and two together and coming up with four. A no-brainer, how could Mum love someone who had been so horrible and hurtful to her for so long?

'Darling,' Mum continued tenderly, 'I love all of my children just the same. I could never love one of you more than the other.'

'But Melissa?' I interjected.

'It's Melissa's behaviour I don't like sweetheart, Melissa is my daughter, just like you are. Sometimes, lately I don't like her behaviour very much, *not much at all really*, but I'll always love her.'

This puzzled me somewhat. Mum and Dad were the centre of my world. When they hurt, I hurt. When they were attacked, I felt attacked. I believed absolutely, they were the wisest people alive and I believed that they had all the answers and an unending supply of knowledge. It was for this reason that I took what Mum said unquestioningly as absolute fact and filed it away. That was that, it didn't matter what Melissa ever said. Mum was always going to love her, and she was always going to be there for her, because she was her mum, and that's what mums did. I had to wonder whether Melissa was aware of this fact too, and if she was, I thought that she had no reason to ever treat Mum better. It was all very confusing and hard for me to understand.

Life continued in a fairly predictable way for another year or so with the eternal emotional ups and downs played out over and over again in the household. Ups and downs that I now attribute to the hormonal swings of an over sensitive teenage Drama Queen, until the day when Melissa went that bit too far, even for her. Some things, once said, can never be unsaid.

Melissa was now eighteen years old and in her final year of school. Her behaviour, both inside and outside the house, had deteriorated even further, if that was at all possible. The police had been involved on more than one occasion, due to unacceptable public behaviour. She had been let off with a warning, but they were watching her, and according to them, the next time she would not be so lucky. Melissa now had no respect for *anyone;* not the police, not the people she worked part-time for, not her teachers, not even for Dad. She was always getting into trouble. She didn't seem to think that there was a problem in that she hated everyone in her life. She had a perfectly plausible explanation as to why it was always the other person's problem. It was because, according to Melissa, they were all '*unreasonable pigs*'.

During this time Melissa's main focus of attack however was on Mum. One day, in an attempt to hit her target fair and square in the heart, Melissa let fly. This time with practiced precision, she taunted Mum until an argument began. She now knew the exact buttons to push to show maximum disrespect. Mum would usually ignore the taunts, but not this day. Mum responded assertively, directing Melissa to stop swearing and yelling in the house and to show a little self-control, to no avail. Melissa continued, there was no stopping her. She told Mum that she was a horrible person, and that nobody liked her. She said she was selfish and only cared about herself and that everyone could see what a bad mother she was. She said that Mum thought she was so wonderful because she looked after the sick children who were dying. Melissa then took aim and followed up with a verbal blow that would never be retractable. With all the venom and hatred she could muster, she spat at Mum how she wished it was Mum who was dying a slow and painful death from cancer, not those innocent children, because it was Mum who deserved to die.

Mum did not know I was in the room, I had come in when I heard Melissa screaming. I could not believe what I had just heard, and for the rest of my life I will never forget the look on my mother's face. It was a look I had never seen before or since. It was a look of shocked disbelief and enormous sadness. She just stood there for what seemed like an eternity without saying a word, staring at Melissa. My world seemed to stand still as I wondered what was going to happen next. After the silence Mum said just two words to Melissa in a monotone voice that was hardly audible and sounded like it had come from someone else, 'Get out'. She then turned and went to her bedroom.

This was the only time I ever saw Dad really lose it. He was enraged after I told him what Melissa had said to Mum. Dad went on a tirade the like of which I had never seen. Ranting and raving, pacing backward and forward like a caged tiger, as though he didn't know what to do next.

'I have had just about enough of her, who the hell does she think she is?' He bellowed. 'How dare she speak to her mother like that, where the hell is she, Sarah? Just wait till I get my hands on her. If that's what she thinks, she can stay out.' Dad stormed into the bedroom to comfort Mum, yelling behind him, 'If she has the nerve to come home, you come and get me straight away!'

I could only hear snippets of their conversation, but I think Dad was cross that Mum had chosen not to tell him herself. I think this was Mum's way of trying to protect Melissa, even after everything Melissa had said. Mum knew that Dad would be really protective of her and incensed over what Melissa had said. She knew he would think it unforgiveable, and she was right. I could hear words like 'ungrateful', 'little so and so', 'who does she think she is?' 'How dare she' … and a couple of other things I should not repeat. I had never heard Dad as angry as he was that day.

Mum did not come out of her room for hours. When she did it was obvious she had been crying. I gave her a hug and told her I loved her and that she was a good mother, but I sensed something was different. I think something inside her broke that day and would never be the same again.

This time Melissa had gone too far, and I think she knew it. She at least had the good sense to stay at a friend's house until the dust settled. Three days later she came back into the house as though nothing had happened. But something *had* happened. I could see it in Mum's eyes. She couldn't bring herself to look at Melissa at the start. Sure, Melissa had apologised, and I think she really meant it, but like I said, some things once spoken aloud can never be retracted. They are out there forever, in the *ether*.

I think Mum forgave Melissa, because that's just who she is, but I don't think she ever forgot. I'm not sure a mother can ever forget hearing those words from her own child. Out of the mouth of someone she has given birth to, someone she has loved, cared for, protected and cherished. You see, my mother was many things, she was a nurse, a friend, a wife, an aunt, a sister, a volunteer for charity, but most important of all for her, first and foremost she was a mother. If she thought she had failed in this most important of things, then nothing else mattered. Success as a mother was how she measured her success as a person. It was due to her commitment to her family and her unconditional love for us all, even when we were horrible or hateful that I knew that being a mother was one of the most important jobs in the world. This is how my whole reality was formulated. This knowing shaped the person that I was to become later in life. I too wanted to have that kind of commitment. I too wanted to be a mum, the same kind of mother as my own, and I never considered, not for one moment, that I would not be.

CHAPTER 2
THE SCHOOL YEARS

During my secondary education I attended a local Catholic secondary school, St Mary's School for Young Ladies, which was run by the Holy Sisters of Charity. Although we weren't strictly practicing Catholics in the sense that we didn't regularly go to church, except for Easter Mass and at Christmas, the fact that I did have five brothers and sisters was usually a bit of a giveaway. The long-standing joke from acquaintances as I grew up, always amidst riotous laughter of course, was '*wow, six kids! What, are you lot Catholic or something?*'

Yes, to all those comedians, I have heard it all a thousand times before, and guess what? It's actually not that funny. The fact remained however, Mum did what all good Catholic's are supposed to do, she did indeed go forth and multiply.

Growing up in a good Christian household with a Catholic school's influence, I soon came to understand the church's teaching on such matters as pre-marital sex and God forbid birth control, there was to be none of either.

Mum and Dad were not so uncompromising on such matters though, Mum believed in the use of birth control, *who would have guessed with six kids*? She had seen too many young girls get themselves into trouble over the years. Don't get me wrong, my parents in no way condoned pre-marital sex, especially with regard to their own children. Their view was when the time was right, and when the right man came along, birth control was perfectly acceptable. Note: I did say birth control only. Pre-marital sex, well, that was another matter completely.

Dad had made it perfectly clear to any boy that came to take me out, that anything they did to his little girl, he would do to them. It was quite a threat, and it definitely had the desired effect. Most of the time the boys were terrified to even kiss me. The thought of Mr Johnston giving them a big *tonguie* was enough for them to keep their lips and their tongues to themselves.

This served Dad well, that was of course until Tony Zorelli came along. Tony was a good Italian boy from a good Italian Catholic family in the area. He was also incredibly hot, and whenever I was near him, my heart started to beat so fast I was sometimes afraid I might faint. When he spoke to me, I blushed so much I wanted to shrink into the floor. He didn't seem to notice though, or perhaps he did, because he asked me to partner him to the fifth form dance formal. Oh my God, my dreams were about to come true. Tony Zorelli was asking me to the formal. I couldn't have been happier even if I had just got straight A's in all my mid-year exams.

Tony did not go to my school, naturally. He attended the local boys Catholic school; St Mark's Catholic College. Back in my day the Catholic school system was quite happy to have segregation of the sexes. Most of the time we were not allowed to fraternize with the boys from the neighbouring school, but the annual combined school formal was the much-anticipated exception to this rule. At any other time, the penalty for such behaviour was to be feared. Once I remember Melissa had to sit outside Sister Rose's office; the Principal, for a whole week because she had been spotted holding hands with a St Marks boy after school, while in school uniform.

The nuns told us that it was difficult enough for young ladies growing up with all the hormones, which were always spoken about in hushed tones, coupled with the general pressures of life and school, such that the added sexual attractions and flirtations of teenage boys was something that should be avoided, always. The Sisters told us there was definitely no room for such distractions in a "responsible" school system. This was possibly a good thing, except I must say from personal experience, that I spent a whole lot of time during my fifth form math and science class daydreaming and trying to figure out how to meet boys, instead of focusing on the logarithmic or scientific equation that was front and centre on the blackboard. This was of course until the fifth form school dance of 1977.

St Mary's, my school, shared this grand occasion with St Marks, Tony's school. We practiced for eight weeks prior to the big event. It was a formal, so we had to learn some ballroom dancing. We learned the foxtrot, the waltz and the quickstep, which was definitely an opportunity for a good laugh, especially when Ricky Stevenson got his feet in a tangle, fell flat on his face and slid right across the highly polished St Mary's Hall floor. His not so elegant quickstep slip came to an abrupt and unceremonious halt somewhere tangled in the underskirts of Sister Rose's habit, but not before knocking poor Sister Catherine flying, to the riotous laughter of all the students present. Ricky, on the other hand was not laughing when he finally untangled himself from Sister Rose's undergarments, he was immediately escorted unceremoniously out of the building, by the ear as I recall, and told not to come back.

As much as the good Catholic girls from St Mary's quite enjoyed the formal dance steps, many of us preferred the more "anything goes but don't dare touch each other", type of dance move that was popular of the times. Naturally there was also the *slow* dance which really just consisted of a kind of stand-up hug combined with a slight side to side foot shuffle, which was slightly awkward, especially to the uninitiated. This more intimate dance was naturally only ever reserved for that special someone and definitely frowned upon by the Sisters, which made it even more appealing. The salsa was also seen as completely unacceptable and far too provocative for *nice* girls, by Sister Agnes who was in strict control of the dance selection and all other such matters.

It was now the late 70's, colour TV was in many homes in Australia, and watching the Tony Bartuccio Dancers on the Don Lane show had become a favourite pastime for many teenage girls with dreams of themselves one day spinning around the dance floor with the boy of their dreams. Now, fast forward to the fifth form formal; it was the best night of my life. Tony danced like John Travolta straight out of *Saturday Night Fever.* Immediately my heart was taken. I would never love another, or so I thought at the tender young age of seventeen. This boy was perfect. *He* and *I, me* and *him, forever.* Teenage love is so desperate and so enormous. You think your heart will break if you lose each other, but you know you *will* never lose each other, because destiny has brought you together, and nothing could ever tear you apart. The total commitment of teenage love which is not tempered from hurt or mistrust, that is honest and real, can so easily be crushed if entrusted to the wrong person at the wrong time as I was later to learn.

The night of the formal was a night I would never forget, it was wonderful. It was as if I was the only girl in the room and all I noticed was Tony. The night progressed quickly and mercifully, after the ballroom dancing was finished, there was thirty minutes of specially selected Chart music that Sister Agnus deemed appropriate. I think one or two tunes slipped under her radar though, and so it was that Tony and I found ourselves slow dancing to the music of Andy Gibb singing "I Just Want To Be Your Everything" and it really felt as though Andy was singing directly to us. I know Tony felt it too as he pressed his body against mine when the ever-present eyes of the Sisters were averted. Could the night have been any better? I soon discovered it could.

Tony Zorelli, the first boy to ever risk the wrath of Mr Johnston, swept me further off my feet when he slowly and ever so tenderly kissed me. It was probably very fast, it was certainly perfectly timed at the exact moment when the attention of all was once again directed toward poor Ricky Stevenson. He had once again managed to get his feet in a tangle and this time landing fair and square on top of his unsuspecting partner-in-dance Susan Baker. As all eyes were on Ricky, Tony immediately took the opportunity to press his lips against mine. The feeling as his lips touched mine was like an electric charge that surged through every cell in my body.

I was infatuated with Tony and I could think of nothing else. I spent the following weeks wondering what he was doing and if he was thinking of me too. Perhaps, the Sisters were right because the order of my priorities had most definitely shifted. Tony had zoomed right to the top, occupying my every thought and math, science, biology and chemistry had slipped right down to the bottom. I spent my school hours gazing out the window and hoping against hope nobody would notice that the lights were on, but nobody was home. My father was beginning to notice the glazed look I had been sporting for several weeks and was beginning to suspect Tony was not as innocent as he appeared to be, and he was right.

It was exactly four weeks and five days and several hours later, when I chanced to see Tony, the love of my life, kissing Melissa Green, the local high school's *sure thing*, behind the bus stop outside my school. That was the moment I discovered that my whirlwind platonic romance with the love of my life Tony Zorelli was over forever.

My heart was broken.

Boys became less important to me over the following years. I never really got over the betrayal of Tony Zorelli. I had fallen for my first love so hard, so fast that the thought of having my heart broken again was too much to bear for a young naïve seventeen-year-old who thought the world would surely end because of this epic betrayal. I naturally tried to make it all Melissa Green's fault, but as time went on I began to realise just what a dead-set scumbag Tony really was. I even found myself feeling sorry for Melissa the day I saw Tony had already moved on to the next unsuspecting girl; Pamela Turnbull, St Mary's School Sports Captain. Poor Pamela - someone really should have told her, but she probably wouldn't have listened. I sometimes wondered what ever happened to Tony, I suppose by now he's on to his second marriage, perhaps third.

CHAPTER 3
MEETING MATT

My chosen course of study was teaching, which was heavily endorsed by the nuns for those girls who were going on to further education. Most young ladies of the time who attended St Mary's, if they ever made it to sixth form, were encouraged to not worry too much about further education, after all, we were all to get married and become stay-at-home mothers, so the Sisters told us. My best friend at school, Jane Robertson, was an exception to this rule. Always the rebel, she refused to be pigeonholed into either typing, secretarial work, nursing or teaching. She wanted to be a trailblazer, she wanted to be a paediatrician. Most of us did not even know what that was, but Jane was a rule breaker and she wanted to go where no other St Mary's girl had gone before. That of course may have had something to do with the fact that St Mary's College for good Catholic girls only went to form 5. So, Jane and I found we had no option other than to take ourselves off to the local high school, the sworn enemy of St Mary's girls, in order to complete our last year of our secondary education alongside my forever nemesis Melissa Green.

The HSC year was challenging enough, high pressure, exams, study, raging hormones, uncertainty about the future, but all this was compounded by the fact that we were most definitely the outsiders. We were considered by most to be those weird lesbians that used to go to the all-girls school. Jane found herself in more than one scuffle over the taunts and name calling we both endured. I chose to ignore the taunts, on the outside at least, and flew beneath the radar. They gave up on me after a while because they never got the response they were looking for and I must have become boring, so I was finally left alone to endure the remainder of that excruciating year. That year felt like it was never ending, but when it finally did, Jane and I reluctantly and tearfully went our separate ways as we both embarked upon the next exciting part of our own education journeys. I began studying at the Melbourne Catholic Teachers College, and Jane who was the form 6 dux was accepted in to Melbourne University, Department of Medicine. She had done it and I was so proud.

Our next adventures were set to begin.

We continued our friendship throughout the university years and beyond. I became a teacher at the local primary school and spent my days surrounded by noisy children and wondered all the while just what it was going to be like when I became a mother. Children liked me, and I liked them, just as I knew I would, motherhood for me would be an easy transition.

Jane, as always, did exactly what she set out to do, she became a successful doctor, but instead of being a paediatrician as she had always hoped, she decided that obstetrics and gynaecology was where her true calling was.

We were the best of friends and we shared everything over these years. Our friendship was one that could survive anything that the world threw at us. It was Jane that introduced me to Matt, and that changed my life forever. Jane was never very interested in men, she always jokingly said that she was already married to her work, and so it was, we were the best of friends.

Life was good!

It was now 1987 and I was twenty-seven years old. I was teaching grade 6 at the local primary school and Jane was working at the Queen Victoria Hospital as a young registrar. The night I met Matt was one that may never have happened except for the fact that late after work one cold Friday winter's evening after parent teacher interviews, my car would not start. Not knowing much about '*car things*' and feeling cold and tired and ever so slightly annoyed, I did what all damsels in distress do, I called my best friend. I really should have called my brother Peter who now was running a successful business as an auto mechanic out of the local petrol station, however my first instinct was Jane. I suppose I really didn't want the grief I expected I would get from my older brother about *girls* and 'how come they know nothing about engines'. Oh, and of course the part about 'I told you Sarah, that car needed a service months ago'. After the longest day of unhappy parents who can't understand why their little geniuses are not at the top of the class, and why it is they only got a C+ instead of an A in sport despite the fact they can't tell a cricket ball from a football, I was left feeling Jane was the easier option. Jane was always the easiest option and naturally she came to the rescue as expected calling my brother on the way, who she directed to come and sort out the whole mess the next morning. You just didn't argue with Jane, she had an authority about her that people instantly recognised, and just quietly, I know Peter always had a soft spot for her although Jane never really noticed it, nonetheless, my mess was sorted.

Shortly afterwards, Jane appeared in the school carpark and rescued me from the seven degree Melbourne winter's evening.

'Jump in,' she said. 'We'll pull past your place, so you can grab some things, you're staying at my place tonight. We are going out.' She spoke with authority.

I always found it easier to agree with Jane, I have never, and suspect *will* never win an argument with her and to be honest, I was too tired to try that night.

It was about eight by the time we pulled up outside Leo's Italian Restaurant, the best Italian cuisine outside Roma itself. Starving, we chose the family size capriccioso pizza. Oh, my God, prosciutto, artichokes, salami, black olives, cheese, who could wish for anything more? I felt sustained after two pieces but pushed it to four combined with two glasses of shiraz. Finally, I felt comfort. I was happy to go home and forget about the day and finally sleep. Jane had other ideas.

Both of us were single at the time, well Jane always was but I had experienced a string of short relationships over the years, all of which ended amicably, none of which really set my heart on fire. I suppose I was looking for that mind-blowing kind of love at first sight elation that you get with a first love, but it seems that was not to happen. I'm unsure if you can ever feel that intensity of feeling ever again, the kind of electricity that shoots through your body after a chance touch as skin brushes over skin. Perhaps, such wonders are only reserved for that first teenage love, I wasn't sure.

What I was sure of was the ever-present questioning from Mum as to when was I going to find a *nice* man, settle down and get to work on her grandchildren. 'Mark was nice. What was wrong with him?' she would gently ask. Mark was my last dalliance. My clock was ticking apparently, I was only twenty-seven years old. People have babies when they are in their forties for God's sake.

Mum, at this stage, was gifted with grandchildren already. Peter's wife Jenny had my three gorgeous nieces; Alisha, Chloe and Rachel, who I love more than life itself. Rick was separated from his wife, this was the "family shame," except for Melissa that is. You were supposed to stick together for the sake of the children, even if you had discovered your wife was having an affair with the next-door neighbour, in your own bed for the last two years. Poor Rick, he did however manage to provide Mum with grand-daughter number four before the break. We don't see that much of Cathy, as she lives with her mother in Queensland, but Rick gets up there every few months. Even the twins Karen and Billy have both had their first born and Karen is already pregnant with number two. She jokingly says she can get pregnant if she just thinks about sex. Interesting concept. Billy on the other hand is not married, I think he must have missed the whole Johnston family 'no sex before marriage' talk. It was somehow more acceptable to Dad because he was a man, his son, so somehow this was okay. Oh, the injustices of being a woman in the 80's, it really was not fair.

Melissa on the other hand was a free spirit. She never liked children, she was none too fond of me or the twins and made no bones about it. I often wondered if it had something to do with the dysfunctional relationship she and Mum had endured in the early years. Whatever the reason she was never to be tied down by conventional relationships. She believed in free love and flower power and was heavily influenced by *Woodstock*, and even though only seventeen years of age at the time, way back in August of 1969, the legendary legacy of this era was to shape her life forever. Mum would be waiting for her grandchildren from Melissa for a long, long time to come. Melissa was now thirty-five. If my clock was ticking was Melissa's even working at all?

I think the point was that Mum really knew, as I did, that I would be the kind of mother that she was. She understood that mothering came naturally to me, and she wanted me to feel complete. My future was predetermined a long time ago, way back when I was five, pushing the twins about in that pram and oh, so, carefully tending to their needs, or perhaps it was before that. I actually believe some things are genetic. Some things you don't choose, they choose you. Now all I had to do was find myself the man of my dreams and all would be well.

As Jane and I left Leo's with a belly full of pizza, we made our way to the Village Cinemas. *Moonstruck* was still playing, it had been on for a few months now and neither of us had seen it. I quite liked Cher and Nicolas Cage was cute, so it seemed like a good choice. Unfortunately, the next session wasn't till 10:45 and I had to confess, I really didn't think I could make it through the one hour and 42 minute film, at that time of night. Of course, I said I was happy to try, but Jane would have to take her chances that the silence of the cinema may be shattered at the most inappropriate of moments by the not so dulcet sounds of me snoring. Decision made, we would go to Gregory's, the local tavern for a quick night cap and then go home.

Gregory's was an intimate little local tavern that specialised in blues music both live and recorded. Some nights the sounds of Matt Taylor on harmonica, John Mayall on guitar or some Billy Joel during his blues stage, would play out in the background as patrons got very mellow, sipping the beverage of their choice in front of the cosy open fire while forgetting the cold Melbourne winter eve outside. On Fridays and Saturdays, local wannabe blues musos from all around would come and play. They got no money, just the satisfaction and love of playing and the hope they would soon be discovered kept them coming back.

This particular night Gregory's was buzzing to the sounds of some new talent playing slide guitar and a cover of Stevie Ray Vaughn. A fairly impressive talent; I remember thinking *he'll go far*. The main area of the tavern was quite smoky, especially when it was crammed full. I have to admit, that was a part of the Gregory's scene that I did not find enjoyable. We grabbed our drinks and made our way to a quiet corner in the back room, away from the crowds and the smoke.

I sat down with my fluffy duck, a personal favourite of the time and Jane followed with her cider. The music was entertaining, but Jane and I were more engrossed in conversation about our respective weeks at work and for me at least, it was the long-awaited weekend. Jane, on the other hand, was rostered on the following night at the hospital to cover the accident and emergency department. 'That's tomorrow,' she happily said. 'I'll worry about that then.' She had a knack of not worrying about tomorrow or anything for that matter, and just enjoying what she was doing now. I always envied that ability, sometimes I wondered if that's what you needed to do in order to work in A&E when you were never quite sure just what was to come through the door next. Perhaps, it was a form of self-preservation, I was pondering this thought … and, the interestingly handsome man across the room who had caught my eye … when I realised he was looking directly at me and smiling. *Oh, crap*, I thought. *Crap, crap, crap*. He saw me staring at him—I immediately blushed and averted my eyes—but it was too late, he began to walk towards us.

Jane was sipping the last drops of cider out of her glass and was unaware of 'interestingly handsome' heading our way. So, I pretended not to notice, but as he stood at our table and leaned right in sporting a cheeky self-assured kind of smile, I had no choice but to look up and meet his gaze … again. His eyes were piercing and the most amazing shade of blue I have ever seen. In that moment, he seemed to see right through my façade, right through to the core of my being. Jane had also now become aware of his presence and immediately jumped up and gave him a big hug. Okay, now I was confused, he wasn't coming over to see me at all. Jane spun around and excitedly introduced me.

'This is Matthew,' she said, 'we go way back.'

'Matthew this is my friend Sarah, I told you about her. Sit down and have a drink. How are you? I thought you were working in Queensland?' Her words were flowing faster than he could answer and he just smiled with amusement.

'Nice to see you haven't changed a bit,' he said.

Jane replied, 'Stay, we have so much to catch up on. What are you drinking? Sarah, same for you?'

And then she was gone, and I was left alone with 'interestingly handsome'. A few seconds of awkward silence was broken by Matthew who then confidently took the lead and started asking me about work, life, and *my* piercingly blue eyes.

Are you kidding? I thought. *A man who notices the colour of a woman's eyes.* I could see why Jane liked this one, but it was strange that she had never mentioned him before. It seemed that she had certainly mentioned *me* to him.

The evening quickly progressed and very soon I knew all about 'interestingly handsome'. He was a physiotherapist who Jane had met at university. They often hung out together in the same group of people. Their paths had crossed a few times after university, the last time being at the Queen Victoria Hospital. He had been working in the physiotherapy department for a few years and was leaving the Queen Victoria Hospital to work in Queensland just as Jane was beginning her residency. Eighteen months later, he came back to Melbourne to start his own business, which apparently was hard at the start, but now beginning to slowly resemble a *growing* physiotherapy practice.

'These things take time,' he said.

I believe they are most often built on word of mouth too, but according to Matthew, it was all going to plan. He was quite the entrepreneur apparently, and he was nice too.

It was Jane that arranged our first date, with the same certainty that she arranged everything.

'Hey, you two should go and see that movie we couldn't get into tonight,' she continued, '*Moonstruck'*, have you seen it Matt?

'No.'

'Perfect. Sarah really wanted to see it. Are you doing anything Sunday?'

'No.'

'Great!' Then Jane turned to me, 'Sarah, all good? Excellent … It's a date then, you'll have to tell me about the movie.'

So it was arranged; Matt and I, this blue-eyed man who I had only just met, were off to the movies. I'm not sure who was more surprised - Matt or me. Jane told me on the way home that I will really like him, he's a great guy. After that first piercing look, I was not going to disagree. It would be interesting if nothing else.

We never really looked back after that first Sunday night; from that date we were an item. Jane knew we would be, and like I've said before, you never win an argument with Jane, so no point in trying. I just went with the flow, after all it was just the movies.

We didn't ever see *Moonstruck* though, session times led us to see a movie called *Raising Arizona*, which I thought was a comedy, but it ended up being a crime movie with a few laughs thrown in for good measure. Perhaps not the best choice for a first date. It was all about an unlikely couple who met, married and couldn't have children, so they stole one.

There were laughs of course but also a lot of language and that poor baby was put in all sorts of dangerous situations, guns firing, car chases, you name it. I remember thinking how sad that someone would feel the need to do such a thing. Matt laughed at my concerns about the poor baby and my perplexed concern over how anyone could ever put a baby in such peril. He somehow found my concern endearing, so he laughed and teased me about it even more despite my indignant protests.

'It's just a movie … but, I do love your maternal instinct.' He then pulled me closer to him and ever so tenderly kissed me.

Zing … and there it was; the fireworks I'd been waiting for, there was one more look into those amazing blue eyes and I knew I was a goner.

CHAPTER 4
THE WEDDING

Matt and I became inseparable over the next few years. Sometimes you just meet someone that sets your heart on fire and you know you will always be together, in fact, it almost feels like you somehow always have been. From that first Sunday, there was a comfort and a connectedness between us that was hard to define. I just knew that this was it—Matt was my forever guy— and I was pleased to quickly learn that he felt it too. Our love was strong, and everyone could see it.

Jane naturally took all the credit for this happy union of souls, while Mum was now quite happy that I hadn't settled for *nice* Mark, who nothing was actually wrong with, except for the fact that I just didn't love him.

Matt quickly became part of the family. He was a year older than me and managed to fit in well with everyone, especially my brothers who immediately allowed him to become part of the famous Johnston family BBQ fraternity. I kid you not, this was almost like a sacred initiation for men in the Johnston clan. The

BBQ was a man's domain, as such no woman was ever to touch the tongs. Sure, the women could make the salads and do all the clean-up, but the actual BBQ was strictly off limits. I'm not sure if this was the culture in other Australian backyards, but it was lore in ours.

The women on such occasions took the opportunity to sit and chat over a glass of wine or two whilst nibbling on cheese and nuts all the while secretly loving the fact that they didn't have to cook.

It was on one of these typical occasions, a year or so later, when surrounded by my family and friends, that Matt found himself in a quite unusual situation; standing all alone at the BBQ with the patri-arch of our family, my dad, Johnno to his mates, Bob or Mr John-ston to everyone else. *No time like the present* thought Matt, so beer in hand and feeling slightly nervous, Matt bravely took this oppor-tunity to ask Mr Johnston if he would allow him to marry his daughter. Dad, still ever so slightly intimidating, stood silent for what seemed to Matt to be an eternity.

Finally, he said, 'Thought you'd never bloody ask.' Turning back to the BBQ he followed up with, 'Sounds like that's a question for Sarah, mate.' And with one final glance over his shoulder, he said with a wink of the eye, 'Oh, and congratulations!'

As Dad turned back to the BBQ, a huge knowing smile came over his face. He already knew what his daughter would say. I was a month off my twenty-ninth birthday when Matt and I got engaged. I just had a promotion at school, which made me the grade 5 and 6 year level coordinator. The extra responsibility of this promotion took up more and more of my personal time, but the extra money was a bonus. I spent my hours planning, correcting and writing reports while Matt was busy building his business, we were both saving as much as possible, and life was great. We spent the weekends looking at houses and planning the wedding. Everything was perfect, and we couldn't have been happier. We had our plan in mind and it was all coming together.

Amidst all the searching for our perfect property we stumbled across a gorgeous little old Californian bungalow in the bayside suburb of Aspendale, just a short walk to the beach. It was an old place and needed a lot of work, but we fell in love with it straight away. From the slightly ramshackle veranda you could see the water, and I immediately knew we would spend many summer evenings here sipping coffee or wine and enjoying the company of passing seagulls and the smell of sea air.

Dad said we were buying trouble, and why would we want all that work when we could get one of those newer places down in Edith-vale for nearly the same money, but we were already sold. We had put in our offer which was the asking price, we didn't even bother to bid lower or perhaps we didn't know to, either way our offer was accepted and our sixty-day settlement period began. This would be where we would start our family life together.

We really wanted to save as much money as possible, so we could furnish our first home and move in straight after the wedding. Naturally we didn't already live together before the wedding, it wasn't the *done* thing, well not in my family anyway. Matt had the good sense to keep his opinions on such matters strictly to himself and in doing so, he kept on Bob Johnston's good side, a wise place to be.

As the months passed by, the wedding date got closer and closer and we were now busy planning our honeymoon in a tropical paradise. Any tropical paradise would do, we couldn't decide which but as long as it was warm, we were happy. Travel brochures became my bedtime reading as I dreamed of massages, cocktails by the pool and snorkelling in the azure waters of some amazing location with Matt by my side.

The days and weeks began to blur into each other, there was always something to do or a decision to be made. It was now only ten weeks until the wedding, which had been planned for late September, ensuring that it definitely did not clash with the Australian Football League's Grand Final day. This was not negotiable. Johnno would never have allowed it. To do so was the height of rudeness and completely inconsiderate, he believed. I remember Dad going on and on about how Aunty Jan, Mum's younger sister, and Uncle Russell had dared to do just that during the nail biter in 1964 between Melbourne and Collingwood. Apparently, Mum never heard the end of it from Dad, right up to the day itself when all the men during and after the church service gathered in small huddles trying to conceal from their wives that they were actually listening to the game on their transistor radios. They did quite a good job at their deceptions too, that is until the final quarter with only four points in it, a Collingwood player missed a final chance to goal and every Collingwood supporter in the vicinity let out a unified groan at exactly the same time as every Melbourne supporter let out an even louder elated … YESSS! The game was up. Melbourne won that year of 1964 and the wedding reception went on as planned, however all transistors were confiscated till further notice.

'How ridiculous to even consider such a thing', Dad would say whenever this was raised thereafter. He was unapologetic about his and the other men's actions, and completely unconcerned about the feelings of Aunty Jan. 'If you embarked upon such sacrilege, you got what you got', he'd say. And that was that.

Over the weeks that followed it seemed there was a never-ending stream of last minute things to get done. Invitations to get back from the printers that needed to be addressed and posted out. That of course infers that the guest list had finally been decided. Yes, the nightmare of all weddings; who to include, who to leave out, whose mother's aunty will be offended if they don't get an invitation even though you haven't seen or heard from them in twenty years, every bride or mother of the bride knows this. Then there's the flowers for the bouquets, the church, the reception tables, who will get a button hole, who won't, the seating arrangements, which are nearly as difficult as the whole guest list *'thing',* and on and on it goes. Oh, yes, not to forget the much-anticipated meeting with Father Green that Matt and I had to attend prior to the ceremony. This was mainly so that Matt could solemnly promise that his progeny will all be raised as good Catholics. He took a little convincing on this, given that Matt had been brought up Anglican, but eventually we came to an understanding.

We had endured yet another cold winter, but spring had now come early and there was excitement in the air. Passports were arranged, dresses were fitted, and suits were booked, and we finally settled on the Maldives for our honeymoon destination; a South Asian island country in the Indian Ocean: Tropical Paradise. I couldn't wait. We decided we would stay at Club Med, they took care of everything which was great because neither Matt or I had been overseas before.

The hens and bucks night was scheduled for the Thursday evening prior to the wedding, and both went off without a hitch. Although we had all of Friday to recover, we really didn't want any mishaps. Matt and I both ensured that our respective evenings were fun but still fairly respectable, much to the disapproval, digs and jibes from our closest friends who inferred we were already like an old married couple, and were complete party poopers. Neither Matt or I cared, we needed and wanted to be feeling great for our day. Feeling seedy was not an option.

The morning of the wedding soon arrived and Matt, Roger, his best mate *and* best man, and my brothers got ready at Matt's house while my sisters, Jane, Mum, Aunty Jan and I made ourselves comfortable at mine. Jane arrived at seven in the morning armed with champagne and chicken for our wedding day breakfast. She said the chicken was essential if imbibing at this hour of the morning, she quoted some medical research and said, 'Don't worry, Mrs J, we'll be fine'. Mum nonetheless was walking around with a two-litre bottle of orange juice trying to dilute everyone's glass. She was slightly nervous which was unusual for Mum, but in the end, she gave up and had a rather large glass herself.

Melissa who had been overseas recently, working at some Indian Mission helping to build schools, had made the journey back especially for the wedding. I never really expected my big sister to make it, but there you go, she always had a way of surprising me. My younger sister however was forever reliable. Karen's best friend was a beauty therapist and so the makeup was taken care of, and another friend was a hairdresser who we had booked for ten. All was going to plan.

As the girls were drinking champagne while being pampered, the boys were flexing their muscles during a quick round of nine holes at the local golf course to ward away any nerves. Matt found golf to be the most infuriatingly frustrating game ever, so I'm not quite sure if it was the best choice, but at least, if nothing else, it provided him with an early morning walk around the park to blow away the cobwebs.

The cars arrived on time, the bridal car belonged to Uncle Sid, Dad's brother. He was the slightly eccentric one in the family. He never got married and lived alone, partied a lot and loved his two-tone black and grey 1953 Rolls-Royce. It was a Silver Wraith Touring Limousine with the original red leather interior and it only ever came out on special occasions, so this was quite a treat indeed. This car was the love of his life. He polished and shined it with the utmost care. No one was ever allowed to touch the chrome, and just in case they did, Uncle Sid had a handy polishing cloth on the inside pocket of his immaculately pressed Armani suit.

Uncle Sid always had a soft spot for me, we just seemed to *get* each other. I always suspected that he was gay, although it was never mentioned. It wasn't really allowed in good Catholic families, especially back when my dad and Uncle Sid were growing up. I don't really have an issue with it. I think people are people. God loves everyone, doesn't he? I mean, everyone loves Uncle Sid. I somehow always just had an understanding that this was not something you choose, it was just who you were. Perhaps, Uncle Sid understood that I loved him unconditionally and even though a word was never spoken on the subject between us, there was an understanding that we both knew to be true. I sometimes look back and feel sad that he felt he could not tell the world who he really was, but this was not a day for such thoughts, we had a wedding to get to.

The weather was perfect on that spring Saturday of September, a gentle breeze and an unseasonal temperature of 26 degrees ensured the day went well.

As I entered the church, Dad at my side, I felt like a princess. My dress ornately adorned with lace, beading in the form of faux pearls and layers and layers of tulle and under skirts that swished with my every step as the two-metre train trailed behind me. It was 1989 and the size of the dresses were only eclipsed by the size of the hair-styles. Perms were the thing and mine was stunningly big.

As I swished into the church, I got my first glimpse of Matt standing with Roger and Peter to the side of the alter. I hardly noticed Roger and Peter, my gaze went straight to Matt's magnificent blue eyes and I was instantly reminded of the first moment we met. He looked so handsome standing there in his black morning jacket complete with tails accompanied with a bow tie and waistcoat, I thought my heart would explode. I was filled with a nervousness and excitement that flowed through every cell in my body, like an electric current, and I hoped against hope that I wasn't about to faint. The rest was a bit of a blur until the moment Matt, standing beside me, slipped his hand into mine and an immediate calm replaced the other feelings and I knew I was safe, everything was as it should be.

The service continued on without incident, I did not faint, and nobody objected to our union. I still wonder why they ask that question, surely if someone had good reason that these two should *not* be married, they wouldn't leave it until then to say. Anyway, out we went to the traditional recessional music, rice and confetti was thrown but *only* when we were outside of the church on strict instruction of Father Green, and finally we were married!

The reception was so much fun. Dad made a wonderful speech, welcoming Matt officially to the Johnston Clan and handing over to him the spiritual and emotional care of his beloved daughter. He reminisced about stories of the past and said things that brought a tear to my eye and an embarrassed rosy glow to my cheek. I think he even made reference to the fact that it was about time for us to increase the size of the Johnston family and bring some more joy into the world in the form of a baby, as only a dad can do on such occasions. Okay Dad, no pressure, let's get to the honeymoon first. The fact that our baby would actually not be a Johnston but would in fact be a Murphy was a small detail my larger than life father had chosen to overlook at that moment. Matt's best man Roger made a speech which was short and sweet, we cut the cake and did the bridal waltz and when the formalities were over everyone let their hair down and it was better than I could have ever imagined. I laughed, I danced and by the end of our amazing day my face actually ached from smiling so much.

Our wedding night was probably similar to that of many other newlyweds; slightly anticlimactic. We made our way, courtesy of Uncle Sid's magnificent Roller, to our wedding night accommodation at The Grand Hotel Chester which was situated just a stone's throw away from our reception venue. Our day had been enormous, and with all the last-minute preparations and wedding nerves I'm not sure I had slept much at all in the previous forty-eight hours. So, it was probably no surprise that on arrival into our wedding suite we both looked at the complimentary bottle of champagne that was provided and the beautiful card attached congratulating us on our union as husband and wife: Mr and Mrs Murphy, which seemed so strange, but it was the bed that at that moment was so much more appealing and not for the reasons you may imagine. I quickly freshened up, slipped on my ever so carefully chosen, wedding night, sexy negligee and as my body collapsed onto the softness of the bed, the combination of lack of sleep and hours of dancing took its toll. The complete relief and comfort of the moment as my whole body seemed to just breathe a welcoming sigh of relief was overwhelming.

Seconds later I was asleep.

Matt ever so gently pulled the covers over me, smiled and crawled in beside me, completely content to just lay with his bride for a whole night.

CHAPTER 5
A NEW LIFE BEGINS

I woke early on that Sunday, the first day of our married lives together, to the sound of rain. I looked over at this handsome man lying beside me and I could hardly contain my joy. I was married. A smile came across my face that I couldn't control—I was married to this slumbering masculine man asleep beside me.

Matt awoke almost as though he could feel the weight of my stare and he smiled back.

'Good Morning, Mrs Murphy,' he said with a stretch and a broad grin.

'Good Morning, Mr Murphy,' I giggled back at him.

He stroked my face and gently reached over and kissed me.

'Now?' he asked.

'Now.' I replied.

Matt's tender touch was electric. He confidently glided his hands over my body slipping off my nightgown as he gently climbed on top of me. I felt the deepest sense of connectedness at that moment to this man and wondered how it was possible to love anyone so much. All thoughts soon disappeared as his gentle movement awakened and excited my body until that precious moment when our worlds exploded. Pure bliss. Making love with Matt was exciting. We grew closer and stronger in our relationship as we intimately explored each other's bodies and responses. My life was wonderful and only one thing could improve my joy, and that would be to have a child with this amazing man, but not yet.

We set off a day later for the airport to embark upon our honeymoon in the Maldives. Our trip there was reassuringly uneventful, and we happily arrived on time as expected. Our villa was at the water's edge with a balcony extending out over the water. We had an indoor and outdoor bathroom and a Jacuzzi perfectly positioned to observe the passing sea life. We saw stingrays, puffer fish even the unusual looking unicorn fish so called due to the protrusion on their heads, quite bizarre and foreign looking but nevertheless fascinating to watch.

This was indeed paradise and we had chosen well, although I really don't think it would have mattered where we were, we would have been happily content in downtown Clayton South as long as we were together. For two weeks we were completely unrushed. We did whatever we felt like. We spent our days by the resort pool sipping cocktails, reading on our balcony, snorkelling in the azure crystal-clear waters of the surrounding islands and making love in the privacy of our comfortable villa. Our evenings were spent eating the most delicious fresh seafood and exquisite desserts while our nights were enjoyed in the tender embrace of each other's arms. Life was perfect.

Time passed as it always does and all too soon it was time to leave our tropical paradise and head home to begin our lives together as husband and wife. It was interesting to discover that even though this wonderful holiday had come to an end, I was ready to leave, even excited to leave, to begin our life as Mr and Mrs Murphy in our little cottage by the sea.

We arrived home and had a few days to settle in before we both returned to work. We walked on the beach hand in hand, unpacked what we could, and spent the evenings sitting on plastic chairs out on our ramshackle veranda, blissfully happy. We had managed to furnish our house with the basics; our new bed, fridge, washing machine and a few other bits and pieces, but we happily accepted donations from friends and family who just happened to be updating their own furniture at the perfect time for us. We scored an unwanted couch from Roger, a dining table and chairs from Jane, and even a coffee table and spare bed from my brother Rick who was moving in with his new partner and no longer needed it.

We felt very fortunate and grateful to all our friends and it was amazing to see it all just come together perfectly in our little home. Matt and I knew what we eventually wanted, and we were happy to wait till we could afford it, and I suppose that was the focus of the next few years. We had big plans for our little cottage by the sea. We were going to make it into our forever home. We loved our Californian bungalow, ramshackle veranda and all, and we were planning to be here for a long, long time to come.

We set to work, days flowed into weeks and weeks into months. It seemed we spent all of our spare time planning what we would do next. We planned to build an extension out the back of the house eventually, which would be our new living area. We had plenty of land to utilise to do it and I wanted to have a good-sized garden for kids to play in, just as I had as a child. I sometimes stood and imagined the day my backyard would be filled with the sounds of children at play. For now, however, Matt and I just did what we could, bit by bit building our dream day by day. We tried our hands at many things, replacing damaged weatherboards and stumps, sanding floor boards and staining decks. We even pulled down walls and then we filled, puttied and sanded some more. We became closely acquainted with the local plumbers, electricians and chippies as we tendered out those things that were beyond our capabilities, while we continued to do the things we could do.

During the days, I was teaching at school, sometimes with paint still in my hair, to the amusement of the grade 6 class, and Matt continued to build his private practice. In the evenings and weekends, we painted inside and outside until our bodies ached. It was a wonderful time. We were building something special, not just our home, but also our relationship. It was during this time we really learned how to communicate with each other, how to listen and how to yield to another point of view. Sure, we had our disagreements, but we made a pact that we would never let the sun set on an argument and we didn't. Renovating is never easy. Each evening when we had done as much as we could, we would always leave time to sit together, often on those plastic chairs on the balcony wrapped up in a blanket with a drink, and we would talk about our day. Then, and only then, we would collapse into bed exhausted but happy, and do it all again the next day.

Now, I wonder, have you ever noticed how time just has a habit of slipping away when you are not really paying attention? I guess that's what happened to us. It really wasn't until the day that Jane stopped by to see how the renovations were going and happened to ask what I had planned for my thirty-second birthday, which was only two weeks away, that I realised just how fast time was slipping by. *How did that happen?* Matt and I had been so busy with work and the house that we didn't even realise.

It was time to slow down. Matt wanted to go on another holiday for a couple of weeks and have a really good break. It would be the first actual break that we had in over two years since the wedding. We both agreed it was time, so I arranged my annual leave and we planned a ten-night trip to Bali.

The week before we left, Matt and I were sitting outside at sunset on the now renovated veranda happily surveying our handiwork from the comfort of our newly purchased outdoor setting. The weather was warming with the change of the seasons and the sun was setting later these days. There was the promise of warmer things to come in the air that night and as I sipped my chardonnay I noticed how I loved to watch the seasons change. It was then that I realised just how many seasons we had already seen come and go from this very spot, and it was in that moment that I decided it was time to start our family. Sure, there was more to do on the house, and it wasn't the best time at work, three staff were already pregnant and next year would be a stretch from that perspective, but I began to get a sense that we had waited long enough.

That evening as Matt and I sat on the veranda we talked about the family we would have. He always thought he would have a son first then a daughter. He was happy with two. I would be happy with half a dozen, but we would probably settle on somewhere in-between. Matt always just smiled whenever I spoke of having lots of children and he always marvelled at the fact that I didn't already get enough of the kids at school. 'It would do my head in', he used to say, closely followed by, 'stop over thinking it all, Sarah, what will be will be'. And so it was, we would finally start trying.

I went off the pill and while we were in Bali we happily tried and tried some more to get pregnant. Naturally it was completely the wrong time in my cycle, well at least I think it was, I had been on the pill for so long it was hard for me to tell, but we tried anyway much to Matt's delight. 'Practise makes perfect', he'd say with a twinkle in his eye, and so practise we did. Neither of us considered, even for a moment the possibility that things would not go to plan.

CHAPTER 6
THE SEEDS OF DOUBT

W e returned from Bali and got straight back into life as we knew it. Several months passed and Christmas was looming. We had now officially been trying to conceive for months, but neither of us were terribly concerned. 'These things happen when they happen', Mum would say with a smile on her face, although I thought I saw a look in her eye that was familiar to me: a look that conveyed concern. I quickly brushed away these thoughts. What could she be concerned about? Almost as soon as I thought about that I heard her words from the past five years playing in my head. *You don't want to wait too long, Sarah. Your clock is ticking.*

Perhaps, my clock was ticking, but at least that meant the clock was still working, so I put it behind me and set about planning for the end-of-year Christmas pageant.

This pageant was the major event of the year at St Patrick's Primary School. Grade 6 students and teachers alike generally performed acts in celebration of the year that was. The grade 5 class put on a slide show projected up onto the school hall wall and each year level performed a class song that had been practised and fine-tuned for weeks in advance. There are always those very talented and very brave students that choose to do individual performances and last year, a particularly brave graduating grade 6 boy dressed up as Mrs Fletcher, the school principal, and sang Shania Twain's "Man I Feel Like a Woman" to the riotous laughter of all students and the horror of all the teachers present. Now, although, Mrs Fletcher does actually have a sense of humour, somewhere, and a degree of leniency is applied to such situations, new rules strangely applied this year. I suppose, being a principal, you may very well have seen it all before, and the thought that some bright spark would try to go one better this year led Mrs Fletcher to rule that *all* acts need to be approved by her prior to the performance and this was to be my job. So, as I checked the program and ensured all teachers had the performance lists to me well in advance, I was then required to collate all information and get that list to Mrs Fletcher's office one week prior to the big event. When that was done, the next job was to get past Susan, a.k.a. the vulture, always hovering and ready to pounce on likely prey, also a.k.a. the gatekeeper, for obvious reasons. As you may imagine this was not always an easy task. I mean this woman was really scary. Mrs Fletcher's personal assistant was a very intimidating woman. Still, with practised determination, I managed to zig as she zagged and success, I was in the inner sanctum. The principal was seated at her desk, head down and pen in hand.

'Excuse me, Mrs Fletcher, here's the program list you asked me to get for you.' I cheerfully said, as I shot a passing glance over my shoulder at the vulture, who looked annoyed and was hovering by the door.

'Excellent, Sarah, give it to Susan on the way out would you,' she said without even looking up.

Bloody hell. I thought. *Vulture: 27, Sarah:0.* I handed the list to the gatekeeper on my way out.

'Thank you,' she snapped, as she snatched the papers from my hand.

The pageant went as expected with no surprises. All in all, a fairly pleasant event as far as these things go and barely a few days later, the school year quickly came to an end.

Christmas in the Johnston household was always a massive affair. I looked forward to it so much. It was a time when all the brothers and sisters, aunts and uncles, cousins, nieces and nephews, and now grandchildren came together. Each year Matt's parents came to Mum and Dad's place. Matt was an only child. Mum would say, 'what was two more', emphatically, followed by 'of course, they are coming, they are family now', and so it was. There was to be no arguing with my mum on such matters. The Johnston Family Christmas, instead of getting smaller as the kids left home, got bigger and bigger every year, especially as the grandchildren continued to grow in number, and none of us would have it any other way. At last count there were eight grandchildren, some came for lunch, some for dinner and an eclectic mix of aunts, uncles, cousins and great nieces and nephews which really made for a marvellous day. All were welcome, and no one was ever turned away.

I recall one day, as Dad went out for ice, on the Christmas morning, he spotted a homeless man in the local park. He came home and told Mum and she immediately directed him to go straight back and bring him home for lunch. She would never see anyone on their own at Christmas. Dad did what he was told as he always did, he knew better than to argue the point with Mum, especially on Christmas Day, and our homeless "Christmas Sam" never ate so well. The extra present, a box of shortbread biscuits, always under the tree specifically for that unexpected visitor, this year found a home with Sam to his utter delight and gratitude. Naturally Mum made enquiries at the local men's shelter, through her work connections at the hospital, and Sam also got a bed for the evening and future care was ensured.

Christmas Day for me was helping Mum and playing with the kids, I was the cool aunty who they all loved. I could always rely on Uncle Sid to get down on the floor with me and the kids and try to figure out a new toy or how to put something together. He had a way with technology and always came equipped on Christmas Day with a ready supply of batteries, the essential component that when forgotten by parents, could really threaten to produce tears and spoil a child's day. When I look back I realise how special these times were, when Christmas really was Christmas. These were the best of times.

After Christmas, the holidays flew by. Matt and I took the opportunity to do a little more work on the house and before we knew it we were back at work. The first half of the year was fairly uneventful. I was starting to pay more attention to my menstrual cycle, which was now a fairly regular 28 days. Jane knew we were trying to conceive and was very excited. She put in her request, or instruction, I'm not sure which, that she would be a wonderful godparent. She also gave me a quick course in the female reproductive system and when would be the best time to conceive. *Thanks Jane*, I thought. *But I'm pretty sure Matt and I have got this covered.*

Jane, who was now thirty-three years old, was in the middle of continuing studies to become an obstetrician and gynaecologist. She always did exactly what she set her mind to, and right now I was wishing that I had that same determined ability to just get pregnant.

Surely that wasn't too much to ask. After all, it's a perfectly natural thing to do, especially in my family. Even my brother managed to do it when he wasn't even trying. Anyway, it wouldn't be happening to Jane any time soon. 'Still married to my work', she'd say. She didn't seem to have any apparent relationships to speak of and I'm pretty sure I would have known if she did. We used to joke about it but I'm really not sure if Jane even wanted kids. Surely her clock was ticking too, but she didn't seem concerned and if she wasn't worried, and she was a doctor, why should I be worried?

More months passed, I had turned thirty-three, and we had now officially been trying for twelve-months. It was around this time that Matt and I were sitting on the balcony on a beautiful spring evening just after my birthday that I finally broached the subject that was starting to concern me more and more. We hadn't really spoken much about it over the last months. It was just something that I kept track of—after all it was my body, my cycle, my mucous, my periods—and my emotional disappointment each and every time my period was one or two days late and I dared to hope that *maybe this time*—only to have all hope crushed once again.

Whenever I tried to discuss the subject with Matt, he would jokingly laugh and say, 'too much information' as he mockingly covered his ears and loudly yelled 'la, la, la, la', in an attempt to drown out my conversation. 'Don't worry, tell me when there is something to tell me', he'd say as he tenderly kissed me and changed the subject. He had been blissfully unaware of all the little moments of hope which had been shattered by the despair of yet another negative pregnancy test or late period.

This night, however, Matt was different. Perhaps he sensed my concern or maybe it was the waver in my voice as I said, 'Matt, there is something that I really need to talk to you about'.

His smile faded slightly as he looked at me and told me to go ahead. I wasn't sure where to start, I didn't even know if we had anything to worry about, but I did know that I was beginning to get worried. It had never taken Mum more than two months to get pregnant. As for my younger very fertile sister Karen, who by now had three children, well, her biggest problem was trying *not* to get pregnant. All I knew at this point, was I could not keep this to myself any longer. I needed Matt. I needed to confide in him, I needed to be comforted by him and most of all I needed to be reassured by him.

With tears welling in my eyes, I told him I was probably just being silly, and I nearly brushed it away, but he insisted I go on. I took a breath and hesitated, it was almost as though if I actually said it out loud it would make it more real. It would then be something that could never be unsaid, never be ignored again.

I mustered all my strength and continued on.

'Matt, are you aware that we have now been trying to get pregnant for nearly thirteen months?' There, I said it, it was finally out in the open. *Now it was real.*

'I guess we have. I really hadn't given it that much thought. I just thought these things sometimes take a year or two, sometimes longer. Tom from work and Janet took three years to have little Leroy,' he said reassuringly.

'Yes, but they were doing IVF, Matt,' I exclaimed in disbelief. 'That's not a good comparison.'

Matt took a moment and considered his reply. He stopped short from saying the usual dismissive or change the subject kind of comment like 'it'll be okay, Sarah' and instead he just looked at me. I guess he could see the worry in my eyes that had built over the preceding months. He got up from where he was sitting and squeezed in beside me, putting his arms around me as he did, and gently said, 'we are in this together Sarah, if you think it's time to see someone about this, I'll be right by your side'. Just hearing those words seemed to relieve a pressure valve from deep within me and I began to cry. Not because Matt was now listening to me, but rather because of the nagging feeling that I just couldn't shift that was telling me, perhaps, now there was actually something he needed to listen to. Matt pulled me closer, he couldn't stand it when I was hurting, he whispered in my ear, 'I'm sure it will be fine, Sarah, we'll do whatever we need to do, and we'll do it together, I'm right here with you'. There was an unfamiliar tone in his voice that said to me that he wasn't actually sure at all. Perhaps, now, he too was beginning to wonder.

I sobbed and told myself that this is not how it should go, I shouldn't be having this conversation, but the cold hard facts were; thirteen months of trying meant that I could no longer pretend that all was well and that this would just take a little time, as both Jane and my Mum had said. I had to consider the possibility that there may be a problem.

I clearly remember Jane saying it can take up to one year of normal unprotected intercourse to get pregnant. We had certainly had that. Our sex life was a very healthy one partly because Matt had still been joking about with the idea that we need to practise, practise, practise at any opportunity, but mostly because even after six years of being together and three years of marriage we still longed to be in each other's arms. To make love to each other was for us the deepest of connection—a union of souls, a feeling that words can never describe or do justice—we loved each other so deeply, so completely that the bond that was forged and strengthened by the precious intimacy and complete vulnerability of making love, could never be broken. We truly believed we could overcome any obstacle together. 'Tonight, may be the night', Matt would jokingly say with a twinkle in his eye that melted my heart, but as it turned out *tonight* was never the *night*.

The next day I called Jane and told her about the previous night's conversation. I hoped that she would allay my concerns, but instead she said, 'I think that's a good idea, Sarah'. Not the reply I expected to fill me with confidence, but I knew she was right. I made an appointment for the following week.

Doctor Rosina Brown was my general practitioner, she knew the family well, and did her best to reassure me that everything was probably okay, but 'it's always good to come and check, just in case'. We discussed my concerns, our sexual history, the timing of our intercourse amongst other things and we left with a screed of blood tests for both of us, and Matt had to get a sperm test. *Oh, great, he's going to love that,* I thought. Still, we did what we needed to do.

I had to get something called a day 2 FSH and LH blood test done amongst others, which would apparently ensure that I was not menopausal. *Really, was that even possible?* I had regular periods, so I quickly put that to the back of my mind. A progesterone blood test was required to check that I was ovulating properly, and the sperm test, well, I suppose that is self-explanatory. Something was mentioned about their ability to swim. Apparently, sperm are a little like people, some are Olympian swimmers and some never quite made it to swimming lessons.

I felt sure that Matt's would be Olympians, but I guess we would see. Four long weeks and another negative pregnancy test later, we both returned to see Dr Rosina to be given the reassuring news that all results were perfectly normal. Matt's sperm were indeed

Olympians and nothing abnormal showed in our blood tests, which was good.

'So why are we not getting pregnant?' I asked.

Dr Rosina went on, in embarrassingly great detail, to discuss the fertile times in the cycle, and the fact that even if you have inter-course spot on time, a pregnancy may still not occur because the egg and sperm may not even meet up together which obviously is an essential component in becoming pregnant.

I'm not really sure where either would go, and I didn't really want to ask but surely there are not that many places to hide in there. Nonetheless, I'll take her word on that one. Now, if by chance the egg and sperm are officially introduced to each other, they may not like each other, and they may choose not to fertilise on a first date, another rather essential component in the baby making chain of events. I reluctantly began to realise that this isn't so easy after all. So, let's imagine for a moment that against all odds the egg and sperm do meet up, and perhaps they actually like each other and decide to fertilise and form an embryo, the poor little thing then still has to go on an enormous journey that can take days, back down the fallopian tube, providing there are no narrowings or road blocks there, until it reaches the uterus. You may think after overcoming all those obstacles that it would be smooth sailing from there, but no, once in the uterus the little embryo faces other challenges. It has to find the right spot to implant, and at this point, it is a little like "Goldilocks". It's looking for a lining that it actually likes, and not one that is too thick or too thin, one that's just right. Even if Goldilocks finds the perfect lining, the whole effort of getting there may have been too much for this embryo and it may be too tired to even pull back the covers and try to get in, so it just stops growing. If it actually does have the energy to implant it may still stop growing after a day or two because life is unfair and after all that effort it may have a genetic abnormality or some other reason that makes it just stop developing. The poor little thing has such a hard start, I mean, when you think about all those obstacles it really is a wonder anyone *ever* gets pregnant.

'Perhaps, you can see why sometimes it really does just take time,' Dr Rosina said to us. 'There is nothing wrong with either of you that I can see,' she said with a reassuring smile. 'Let's give it another twelve months, if nothing has happened by then, which I'm sure it will have, then we'll do some more investigations.'

We left feeling reassured that all was well and went back to life as usual; however, I was later to realise that this was a massive mistake that I would soon come to regret.

CHAPTER 7
MY BODY'S BETRAYALS

I t was time to get serious, we needed to plan this right and stop messing around. Matt would have to get on board with me now, no more *anytime* will be fine, we had to get scientific about this. I counted my cycle days and started to use urine ovulation tests and even monitored my mucous to detect the perfect time for intercourse. I took my temperature every morning before getting out of bed to observe the subtle changes that may indicate I was ovulating just in case the urine test or the mucous changes missed it, and I found this even more frustrating because my temperature was up and down without a rhyme or reason. 'How could this be accurate?', I complained to Matt who really had no idea how this could be accurate but thought better than to comment on the science of it all.

I was doing more and more complaining to Matt over the months that followed as I became completely obsessed with getting pregnant. Over the next twelve months, even our sacred love making became tainted with my new quick-I-think-the-time-is-right mentality, so much so that I noticed I had stopped calling it lovemaking and started referring to it as *sex*. A term that I had previously chosen never to use because when Matt and I made love it wasn't just *sex*, it was so much more than that. Times were changing.

I became so focused on what to eat and what not to eat, when to exercise, what supplements to take, what shampoos and soaps to avoid, and even what sexual positions were best for getting pregnant. I journaled and diarised it all. Everywhere I turned there seemed to be people advising me on what I should and shouldn't be doing to increase my chances. There were magazine articles, documentaries, and I spent hours at the library doing research on fertile cultures around the world, exploring what they did that made such a difference. I quickly became an expert on the female reproductive cycle, I even started to make Matt wear boxer shorts, instead of tight fitting underwear. This was supposed to help keep the sperm cooler and healthier. Apparently, sperm were happier when they were cooler and so boxers it was. I became obsessed with every detail, and one day, I even recall testing my urine while at work. When I realised I was ovulating, I feigned sickness, left work, raced home to call Matt so that I could order him to come home straight away. No discussion, I was ovulating!

Matt did *not* come home from work that day, my tolerant beautiful husband was beginning to tire of my obsessive ways and the cracks were beginning to show in our relationship. We even began arguing about things that we never argued about before. This wait was taking its toll. I attended two baby showers in that twelve months. One for the grade 3 teacher, Rosemary, and one for the school's secretary. Both pregnant for the first time, both, as you would expect, completely excited and engrossed in their own situations and the growing life inside of them. Both women were totally unaware of how lucky they were and even more unaware of how hard it was for me to watch their pregnancies progress. The third baby shower was for a closer colleague, Julie. We had started at the school at the same time and were good friends, and despite this, I could not bring myself to attend. I suddenly came down with a convenient dose of gastro and stayed home and cried. I began to notice more and more just how difficult it was to be around pregnant women. It was a constant reminder of what I could not do, what I feared I may never be able to do.

I was thirty-four when we finally returned to see Dr Robina and she advised us it was time to do more investigations. She referred me to a gynaecologist, and six weeks later I was having a laparoscopy. This was apparently to check that my tubes were clear and there were no other obvious issues that may have been preventing me getting pregnant. I remember thinking *two years of trying and now they are checking my tubes are clear.* These days I was often vacillating between fear and anger. *This was so unfair. Why was this happening to me?*

Another Christmas was looming and the usual excitement I felt about this joyous family celebration was absent this year. I would have to wait till mid-January for the results of my laparoscopy. Everything seems to shut down over Christmas, and even doctors go on holidays. The wait was agonising. I was beginning to notice how the thought of having to be around my fertile sister's family and my brother's children at Christmas was making me feel something I could not quite define. Perhaps, a cross between anger, frustration, and something I didn't want to admit, jealousy. I knew this was a feeling that I didn't like. *Was I jealous of my siblings? Did I resent their happy families?* Or, did I resent the fact that they could never understand what I was going through? I wasn't sure. All I knew was I had begun to avoid certain people and certain places that reminded me that I was not getting pregnant. This was something that I kept to myself, at least for a while. Matt just didn't seem to understand, but he did begin to notice the change in me.

Christmas came and went. It wasn't the same this year and I wondered if it ever would be again. I didn't get down on the floor to participate in our Christmas ritual with Uncle Sid and the kids to excitedly investigate the workings of some new technology or toy. I chose instead to develop a stress headache and took myself off into the spare bedroom to lie down. Mum was concerned. 'You're working too hard, Sarah', she would compassionately say. She had stopped asking me about the pending grandchildren, she'd suspected all was not well.

It was the middle of January when finally, we got to see my gynaecologist for the results. Instead of feeling rested and relaxed from nearly four weeks of holidays, I was actually feeling completely exhausted and stressed. I had not been sleeping well, I couldn't stop worrying. Thoughts of regret kept going through my head: *Why did I wait so long? Why didn't I listen to Mum? What if I had started sooner? What if I never get pregnant? What if ... what if ... what if?* This was the never-ending conversation in my head that kept telling me over and over that this was my fault.

I attended the gynaecologist visit on my own. Matt was interstate at a conference that was apparently more important than us getting pregnant. We had argued about this, but he went anyway. 'Life has to go on, Sarah', he said as he left.

All of our results once again came back normal. I just couldn't understand why we were not getting pregnant. We were offered something called ovulation induction and timed intercourse. This is where I take a medication to produce a follicle and ovulation is triggered with another medication and we are told when to have sex. *How very romantic* I remember thinking. There was also a mention of IVF, which I immediately disregarded. I didn't know much about IVF, but I did know that none of my family had ever needed to do it, and I didn't want to be the first. These were things I needed to discuss with Matt, and again I felt a twinge of frustration, and resentment that he was not there with me. 'We'll do this together, Sarah', I remember him saying. *Where was he now?* I went home and cried.

When Matt finally did arrive home from his *very* important conference we really didn't need to say much about the next step, we both felt at this stage that we really didn't have much choice. Matt as usual was the voice of reason saying that it didn't matter how we got pregnant, as long as we got pregnant, and so I quickly forgave him for his little indiscretion and the decision was made. We would give the ovulation induction a go.

We were advised to only do four cycles as the ticking of my clock was now becoming deafening, however we were assured by our gynaecologist that given there was no obvious fertility issues we should have good success. After four cycles, God forbid, if we were still not pregnant we would have no choice than to consider IVF.

During this time Roger and his girlfriend of eighteen months Justine, who weren't even married and not even trying to get pregnant, did just that. Roger was ecstatic, he had fallen hard for Justine and she was equally as besotted by him. The day they came to tell us their happy news, Justine was beaming and couldn't contain her joy. She babbled on and on about all things pregnancy, morning sickness and sore breasts. There was no escape for me. I just had to listen for what seemed like forever until the moment she made some comment about when we were going to take the plunge into parenthood too. Deadly silence filled the room. Everyone looked at me awkwardly, afraid to speak and Justine immediately understood the situation. This was a topic of conversation I had always avoided, but why hadn't Roger told her? I could sit no longer. I got up, excused myself, and went into the bathroom and threw up. Matt made an excuse that I was unwell, but everyone knew the truth in that moment.

My relationship with Justine became more distant after that day. Roger used to come over on his own and make an excuse that Justine was busy or resting. I was quietly happy to not have to watch her growing pregnancy in my own home. It was a constant reminder of what I was unable to do. Roger found it difficult to understand how I felt when I refused invitations to their house. He said to Matt 'I was being rude'. Matt would say to me, 'life goes on Sarah', oh, how I was beginning to hate those words. Surely, he of all people should understand how I felt. The fractures in our relationship were growing.

Six months passed quickly and painfully.

Disappointment after disappointment served to make me more and more anxious that perhaps this may never happen for us. I felt like I was falling apart. All I was focusing on was more wasted months with nothing to show other than doctor's bills. I actively spent my time avoiding friends and family who were pregnant. I averted my eyes whenever I saw a mother and baby in the street, my tolerance levels for so many things had reached zero and it seemed that Matt and I were snapping at each other all the time.

I was fast approaching thirty-five. The strain was really showing on us both. The few friends and family who knew we were trying to get pregnant, would say infuriating things to us like 'just go on a holiday and relax'. Supposedly this would miraculously make everything all right. Or 'stop stressing about it and it will just happen' and even more annoying were those who we hadn't told, who would say things like 'your turn next, Sarah', in an irritatingly happy voice as I would be cringing on the inside. 'Isn't it about time you two started a family?', with a knowing wink that made my stomach churn. It was all I could do to stop myself saying out loud the dialogue that was playing over and over in my head: *My God, you are rude and ignorant, why don't you all just go and screw yourselves.* But instead I just smiled sweetly. People, I discovered, were so unaware and inconsiderate. Pregnant women were suddenly everywhere and at times it seemed that there was nowhere to escape, so I stayed home more and more. Mum was now officially worried, and there was no hiding it.

'Sarah, you need to go to that clinic at Monash and talk to a specialist, someone who actually works in this field, not a gynaecologist, someone who deals with infertile women every day, an infertility expert,' she said with growing concern in her voice.

The first time she said it, I brushed it off. *The doctors know what they are doing, Mum.* Now, I'm not so sure. Her words hung in the air, *"infertility expert"*. There you have it, I am an *"infertile woman"*, no longer just a woman, now I'm an *"infertile"* woman. I wished this diagnosis came with a label I could wear around my neck that would say to all the ignorant people, back off! Or, don't ask! Or even, shut up! But it didn't. I knew on the inside Mum was wondering if that clock of mine was still ticking or, perhaps it had been broken all along. She had said this more than once and now all I heard was the harsh grating sound of the words "infertile women". There was no hiding it or denying it any longer. That was me, infertile, yet I still wasn't sure I wanted to go the way of IVF.

I needed time to think. There were ethical considerations after all. This was really messing with things that maybe aren't supposed to be messed with. Was this even ethical?

The voices of the nuns at St Mary's School for good Catholic Girls rang in my ears: *'It's God's will, Sarah.' Was this God's will? Was I actually being punished for something?*

I closed my eyes and shook my head in an attempt to make the thoughts stop, but they wouldn't stop. I wasn't sure IVF was for me, perhaps I should just accept my fate. If God wanted me to be pregnant, I would be pregnant, after all there was no infertility in my family.

I knew I needed time to think but time was definitely against me.

I threw myself back into school life as Matt and I continued our futile attempts to get pregnant on our own. We even did two more ovulation induction cycles, both to no avail. Sex now was officially something that I did not look forward to or enjoy. When I look back this was definitely my denial stage and after another six wasted precious months, Matt and I finally had to accept, it was IVF or nothing.

We chose IVF.

We only told some people we were going to begin IVF. This, for us, was a very personal journey. Until this point I really wasn't sure how I felt about the whole test tube baby thing and I certainly did not need anyone else's disapproval or judgement. I knew that the Catholic church frowned upon it. Something to do with fertilisation happening outside the body and not being natural, and somehow being against God's will. I'm not sure that God wanted me to be childless, and anyway, I rationalised, why would He give these scientists the knowledge and skills to do these things if it really was against His will. Our decision was made, and I tried not to think too much about it.

We had to make a choice as to where to go and who to see, another clinic, another doctor. I somehow felt even more despairing. Matt wanted me to be positive, but how could I? Three and a half years of constant disappointments had taken its toll. I think I was moving into a kind of self-preservation mode. Part of me wouldn't allow myself to hope or believe so that I wouldn't be hurt when the next round of bad news came, but there was another part of me that was beginning to get excited. This was "In Vitro Fertilisation". IVF surely had to be the answer. When people can't get pregnant they do IVF and they get their baby, and we would get ours—I defiantly thought.

There were a couple of large clinics in Melbourne. We chose the one that offered promises of great success. It had many pictures of happy women with babies on their brochures and quoted encouraging figures of how many babies they had helped create. They were apparently world leaders in the field of IVF research and practice, and so I began to feel relieved. Now that our decision was finally made, I allowed myself to feel quietly confident that these world leaders knew exactly what they were doing, and I would soon have my baby in my arms.

CHAPTER 8
IVF

'Our first available appointment is in six weeks,' said the receptionist at the Infertility Specialist's Clinic.

'Six weeks?' I thought, but in fact I must have said it out loud.

'Yes, six weeks is the earliest, you're lucky, we've just had a cancellation, he's a very busy man.'

I didn't feel very lucky.

I was becoming more and more aware that time was now my enemy. What they never tell you at high school and in your early twenties, when many are feverishly trying *not* to get pregnant, is that time is of the essence and should not be wasted. Having children is apparently something that we should not put off until your career is on track; you've got the perfect house and had that holiday you've always wanted.

I was thirty-two when I started trying.

My clock was ticking, and I didn't even know it.

Well educated, nevertheless, here I was, moving quickly toward thirty-six, and my chances of success reduced with each passing day. I knew I wasn't twenty-five anymore, but thirty-five is still young. I felt like I did when I was twenty-five and I didn't look much different.

However, none of that mattered, the truth is that I was fast marching toward being thirty-six and *infertile*.

So, it was six weeks later when we arrived at the office of Professor Tom Peterson. Matt and I sat in the waiting room holding hands, surrounded by other women. I wondered what they were here for. Some were older women, surely they weren't here to get pregnant, and I knew that the kind looking grandma over in the corner certainly wasn't. One woman looked as stressed as I felt, she averted her eyes when another woman with a baby walked into the room. She looked like she was about to cry. I felt so sorry for her and then wondered if that was to be my fate too. Mercifully my thoughts were interrupted by the receptionist calling my name. It was finally time for our appointment.

Professor Tom Peterson had an impressive office, he was seated behind a large mahogany desk adorned with the latest computer technology which was connected to the Internet. It was now 1995 and although the Internet was something I had to use at school it still scared me a little. I didn't understand how it worked exactly so out of school I stayed away from it as much as possible. Happy to leave it to those computer nerds who knew what they were doing.

I brought my attention back to Professor Tom Peterson, who by this stage was staring at me noticing I was more interested in his computer than him.

'Excuse me,' I blushed. 'I'm a little nervous.'

He smiled and said, 'I have read your referral and you've been through quite a lot, haven't you?'

At last, someone who understands.

He looked too young to be a professor, but the slight traces of grey hair hinted that he was older than I thought. I instantly liked him. Perhaps, Professor Tom Peterson was the answer. I felt a twinge I had not felt for some time: hope.

We left the appointment with handfuls of request forms, more blood tests of every kind. Some we had done already but had to repeat, some were different ones. Screening tests, to ensure we didn't have any infectious diseases, blood tests to ensure I was still ovulating, an ultrasound scan to look at my ovaries, tubes and lining. Matt even needed another sperm test. Apparently, the infertility clinic was not happy with tests run by other pathology clinics. They were the experts and they were certainly thorough.

Professor Tom said we also needed counselling. Initially I worried that he could see that this journey had been particularly difficult for us as a couple, but I was reassured that this was a requirement for all. It was not counselling to see if we were adequate parents, it was to discuss all the ethical considerations of IVF. I really didn't want someone telling me it would all be all right no matter what the outcome, especially someone who had no idea what I was going through because I knew if we couldn't have children, it would *not* be all right.

It seemed that once we were in the system we could get an appointment sooner with Professor Tom; however, we still had to wait until all results were back. In the meantime we had registration forms to fill in for the IVF clinic and plenty of other appointments to book. The whole process seemed to take a *long* time.

On our return visit, Professor Tom reviewed all of our results and set a treatment plan in place. He told us that we would need to call our IVF nurse to make another appointment. We hadn't even started the treatment and already I was having trouble fitting all of the appointments in around work. The school is not happy for teachers to have time off, and I have had a lot off already. This was just something else I had to worry about. I was also worried that I was gaining the unwanted attention of "the vulture" who would certainly ensure that the principal was well aware of my absences.

Two weeks later, the day of our nursing interview was upon us. Susan, our IVF nurse, looked friendly and professional. She had worked in IVF for over ten years and she confidently welcomed us as she ushered us into a private consulting room. Our appointment took about an hour and there was so much information that I had trouble processing it all. I hoped Matt was taking it all in.

Susan, who was obviously used to the look of overwhelm that was now emblazoned across my face, said 'I know it seems like a lot of information, but it is all written down in your paperwork and you can call me at any time. Just take it one step at a time, we will guide you through'. I was thinking, *sure, no worries* as Susan looked at us like this was all normal, but I didn't feel *normal*—if we *were* normal we wouldn't have to be telling a stranger about our sex life —if we *were* normal, an IVF nurse would not have to tell us when to have sex. If we *were* normal Matt would not be sitting here having to listen to a young girl telling him when to ejaculate and even worse, how to do it. What was a split ejaculate anyway? To ejaculate into one jar seemed nearly impossible, but to do it into two jars? I tried not to think too much about it and began to refocus my attention back to the bit about when *not* to have sex. The sperm were at their best when the last ejaculate has been between 3-5 days before the egg collection. We *certainly* want the sperm to be at their best. Their previous performance is nothing to write home about, Olympic swimmers or not. My mind just wouldn't stay on track … *is anyone else embarrassed by this conversation? I mean, seriously, who talks about the last time they ejaculated to a complete stranger, especially to a young girl.* I look over at Matt, he's looking at the ground, his cheeks a slight shade of pink, which I've rarely seen before. I'm sure he's hoping she will move on quickly, but she doesn't. She starts talking about the day of the procedure and if Matt wants to produce the sample at home, then, here are the jars, fill in the attached paperwork, do *it* just before you leave home and keep *it* warm until you get to the clinic. She explains that some guys prefer this. *Really? Seriously? Compared to what? Exactly what part of this do they prefer? Stop it!* I inwardly chastise myself. *Focus for God's sake Sarah.* Susan continued on completely unaware of the deafening dialogue playing in my head. If Matt preferred to do the sample at the clinic, a time could be booked. I look towards Matt who without looking up quickly says he'll 'do it at the clinic', hoping against hope that Susan would now move on to something else, anything else and mercifully she does.

We were apparently doing something called a down regulation cycle, and if I was in any kind of a hurry, then I needed to think again. This cycle would take almost two months, and I was to be put on the pill first. *Come on guys, the pill! I'm trying to get pregnant not avoid pregnancy.* But I did as I was told and took the script.

'Who is going to be doing the injections?,' Susan asked with a big smile.

Crap, the injections! Now it was my turn to look panicked. I hate injections, how on earth was I expected to do it to myself? Matt knowing how I felt, offered to do it for me. Instantly my body filled with horror at the thought. Surely this wasn't natural. An image of Matt chasing me around the house with a loaded needle in hand sprang to mind and I immediately told Susan that we'd go to the doctor's. Matt looked slightly offended, but I was in no mood to be warm and fuzzy right now, this was serious.

Unfortunately, I was soon told that going to the doctor's was not really an option, something to do with Medicare and a global fee. It was all too much to comprehend, so I had no choice but to turn my attention back to Susan who was pulling out needles and syringes in front of me. The instant wave of nausea that flowed through my body causing the blood to drain from my face leaving me as white as a sheet apparently went unnoticed and eventually subsided. Fainting may have been a blessing right now, but life is cruel and instead I had to continue listening to Susan droning on about powders and waters. I was expected to mix two powders and one water or was it two waters and one powder, I really wasn't sure. My head was spinning with information. *What if I got this wrong? So much information! God, who injects themselves anyway —other than the obvious—and we won't go there. Focus Sarah FOCUS!*

Thoughts were bombarding my conscious awareness, so much information. *I'll be talked through, step 1 and 2, that's it, just steps 1 and 2, it's all right there on the paper. This can't be too hard surely.* My mind had a life of its own. I couldn't stop the thoughts that were making me feel this way. I wanted to run out of the room, but my legs betrayed me and where would I go anyway? This thing, this *infertility* would come with me, and so I sat and tried to find the hope I was supposed to be feeling right now. Hope that this was the answer, but there was that ever-present feeling of doom in the pit of my stomach that told me to protect myself.

I'm usually very confident but I don't mind saying this was freaking me out.

We left with our "little bag of goodies" as Susan called it. Scripts, drugs, some for the fridge, some for the cupboard. Paperwork, needles, syringes and alcohol swabs. *What if someone sees drugs in my fridge?* I quickly put the thought out of my mind, that was the least of my concerns right now. We were told to call the clinic with the first day of my cycle, and we would be given further instructions from there.

True to Susan's word, it did all just come together. The first injection was the worst, but really it was just the anticipation of it that was terrifying. When it came down to it, it was all a bit anticlimactic, over and done with before I even knew it and surprisingly it was actually easy. So, it was that nearly two months after our nursing interview, I was booked in for my monitoring ultrasound scan. This was to see when we would be timed for theatre. I was now beginning to notice that I was actually looking forward to the egg collection. It had all gone so smoothly that I was daring to believe that this may just work.

On the day of the scan, I was told that I would get a call in the afternoon to tell me what to do next. All day at work I was feeling happily distracted, excitement was building within me and I finally got the call at 3:45. Susan was on the phone, but her voice gave away that all was not well, I braced myself for what was to come. Apparently, I had not responded to the injections. *They* thought I could do better. *They* wanted me to stop the cycle.

I could hear the words, but they were not making sense. *They think I can do better ... it feels like I'm being told to try harder. Is this my fault? Have I failed my IVF test? I've never failed anything before. Matt can't be blamed he hasn't even started his part, it's all me.*

There are no excuses and the reality of this hits me like a severe blow to the stomach that seems to take my breath away. *This is my fault. I have waited too long!*

I am instantly filled with a combination of sadness and remorse. I'm glad school is finished.

I hold myself together until I get into my car and suddenly I can hold it off no longer. As I sit in the carpark, I'm suddenly blinded by a torrent of tears that flow uncontrollably and I hope nobody sees me, but I can't be sure.

CHAPTER 9
BACK TO THE DRAWING BOARD

Another birthday.

Thirty-six.

Childless.

Things were bleak, and as the cold late winter weather continued into what was supposed to be spring, my heart felt heavy with despair. I did my best to carry on as if everything were normal, but my work was beginning to suffer. How could it not? I felt as if my world was crumbling around me and nobody really understood. At times, I found it hard to breathe, the reality of this "infertility burden" was weighing me down and at times I felt as though I would surely drown in the hopelessness of it all. I was also finding it even harder and harder to communicate my feelings to Matt, he just didn't seem to be going through the same emotions as I was, and this made for some very heated discussions. We were arguing more and more. Matt just wanted me to get on with things and start anew as if nothing had happened. 'There's nothing we can do about that, Sarah. Let's just move forward', he would say. Then he would often leave the house and go to Roger's to fix a car or watch the football. I know he felt anywhere would be better than staying around the toxic person that I was becoming. There was a part of me who couldn't blame him, but there was another part of me that hated him for his inability to understand me.

Our once beautiful love life was now officially non-existent. Was this my fault, or was it his? All I know is that neither of us wanted to be intimate anymore. Sure, we tried from time to time just for appearance sake, but something was now broken, and I wondered if it could ever be fixed again. Real intimacy required something we no longer had—an ability to be in that special moment where nothing else mattered except the two of you; a special connection that only you share—instead, it now felt like our special moment was being directed by a whole IVF team. I could never find myself in that space any more where nothing else mattered and so sex now was a constant reminder of the fact that we could not have children and maybe never would.

The next cycle commenced, and we were reassured of a probable better outcome. Our FSH dose was increased to the maximum dose. This fact did not fill my heart with joy. I needed the maximum dose. *Was that a little like flogging a dead horse?* I wondered. *Why was my body not responding and what if it did not respond to this dose? What if I just started trying earlier? What if I only listened to Mum? What if? What if? What if?* My head was spinning with negativity, too many *what ifs*, the sound of it was threatening to deafen me.

I tried to focus my attention on positive thoughts, but I really didn't believe what they tried to tell me. Hope was becoming a painful luxury that I was not prepared to entertain.

Cycle two commenced after more appointments, more money, and more wasted precious time. Here we go again. This time I did have a better response, nothing to write home about, but three beautiful little follicles were present on the day of the scan and even better, they were the right size. I thanked my body for finally getting it right and set about the scary task of taking my trigger injection. No pressure, at all, but this particular injection had to be done at exactly the right time. Too early and I may ovulate before theatre, too late and the eggs won't be released. I had to wonder at the lack of common sense that led to the decision of allowing a hormonal woman with no medical background to take on such a responsibility. I tried to picture the medical meeting where people in white coats sat around a table and said something like 'Yes that sounds like a great idea, let's go with that'. Matt and I took our instructions very literally. We were told to take the injection at 9:30 on Tuesday night, and 9:30 was exactly when we nervously injected it; not a minute early, not a minute late.

Thursday morning, we went to theatre and had two eggs collected. The next day we were to be told only one of them had fertilised. Susan had gently told me 'it only takes one, Sarah. Let's just see how it goes', she'd said it with the compassion of someone far beyond her years who has had to convey this kind of news many times before. Our little embryo did survive until day three, against all odds and I had my little baby embryo transferred.

For the first time in my life I was carrying an embryo inside me. I felt strange; somehow womanly and maternal all at the same time. I knew I had to do everything I could to protect this life within me, and so I took the next two weeks off work so that I could do just that.

The day of the pregnancy test seemed to take forever to arrive and the wait for my results that afternoon seemed even longer. My period hadn't arrived, and I was told this was a good sign. I was also told not to do a urine test as it would *not* be accurate due to the drugs I had been taking, but I couldn't help myself. I did one anyway and it came back positive. I couldn't believe my eyes and I was instantly filled with excitement and joy which made the wait for the official result even longer. Mum and I spent the day together as we waited for that phone call. When Susan finally did call that afternoon, the phone hardly got a chance to ring before I grabbed it. I could not contain the excitement in my voice as I gave her my name and date of birth, but the next words were ones I would not soon forget.

'I'm sorry, Sarah, your result is indeterminate.'

'What?' I said as instant confusion took over.

Susan went on to explain that I had some pregnancy hormone, but it was low.

'It's what we call an indeterminate result,' she said. 'It could go either way.'

There had been an implantation, but the levels were not where they should be.

I hung up the phone and felt as though I'd been punched in the stomach and winded. *What does this mean? Either, I'm pregnant or not pregnant.* Indeterminate was never an option. I turn to Mum with a look of shock on my face. I don't know whether to be happy or sad. 'I'm indeterminate', I say. Mum says nothing at all, she knows exactly what to do. She sits down beside me and hugs me, just like she always did when I was growing up and somehow that makes it better, at least for the moment.

I try not to think of the embryo inside of me struggling to hold on to life, my little baby embryo. I can do nothing but wait, but this time the wait is short, the next day I get my period and the following blood test shows all my levels are back to normal. Normal, even the word now sounds alien.

Matt and I both found this latest experience very difficult to deal with. IVF was supposed to be the answer. I remember friends and colleagues talking to me about putting off their families until they had the career, home or other financial obligations under control. Once I would have felt that this was a perfectly reasonable thing to do. They believed that when things didn't go to plan there was always IVF. They believed IVF was a sure-fire thing, God, how wrong they were. I just wanted to scream from the roof tops to anyone who would listen 'DON'T WAIT!' Why hadn't someone told me that? But then my mind once again went to Mum saying, *Sarah, your clock is ticking.* The thought caused so much guilt and such remorse that I could hardly breathe.

This was all my fault.

Matt and I decided we would go away for a few days to rest and try to make sense of it all.

We went down the Great Ocean Road, with the sun roof open and allowed the wind to blow the cobwebs away. The walks on the beach and the smell of salt in the air was medicine to my soul. Matt felt it too, and for a while we could forget the world and just get back to us.

All too soon we had to drag ourselves back to reality. Our break was just a few short days. It was all we could really afford. Neither of us were ready to say it out loud, but we were both well aware that the cost of IVF was taking its toll in many ways.

Over the next ten months, Matt and I did another three stimulated cycles. We got three eggs on our third stimulated cycle, and none of these eggs fertilised. This was a major shock to us both and even though we were prepared that this could happen, we felt devastated. More wasted time, more wasted money.

We were told we needed to do something called ICSI. This is where they take the sperm and inject it directly into the egg in case the sperm were lazy, or the egg was excessively strong. Even though Matt's sperm looked normal and were Olympic swimmers, sometimes the sperm just don't like the eggs. Something about antibodies was mentioned and I really didn't care about the details. *Just do what you have to do* I thought, but I had to wonder if Matt's sperm always didn't like my eggs, or if they were just sick of my horrible moods now too.

The second cycle during this time was more successful. We got four eggs and three fertilised; we transferred one and froze one.

The one we transferred did not implant and my period came very early. More devastation, and even though I tried not to get my hopes up, it was unavoidable. We embarked on the frozen cycle and that embryo did not even survive the thawing process. *How many things can go wrong?*

Matt and I were now officially struggling. He was trying so hard to be there for me, but I seemed to be in a dark world of my own making and felt like I was drowning in despair with nobody that could throw me a lifeline.

Our fifth stimulated cycle was what they call a "boost" or a "flair cycle". This was a shorter cycle designed to really hammer my ovaries, so they produced more eggs—it worked—the scans looked promising, and on the day of egg collection I got six eggs and four fertilised. This was the best yet.

I allowed myself to be quietly confident.

Perhaps this was it.

We had been advised to grow our embryos on to day five, so they would reach the next stage of their development. They would be blastocysts, and blastocysts, we were told, had a better chance of implantation. So, our four little embryos were watched and monitored each day, and each day one by one they stopped growing. By day five we had one left. We were told that this one had the best chance, so it was transferred, but just like the others it did not implant.

During this time, I had tried just about everything. I had been taking Chinese herbs, going to a naturopath, having acupuncture, massage, detox diets and even seeing a counsellor. Every single morsel of food or drink that entered my mouth was planned and considered. I had exhausted all avenues of complementary therapies, regardless of the costs. I would have even stood on my head and recited the national anthem if they said it would have helped, but nothing helped. The more disappointments I endured, cycle after cycle the more I got involved with an IVF support group. A Group specifically designed to help people like me. Infertile people like me. Unfortunately, this particular group was filled with women who had no success and who were pretty pissed off at the world, just like me. I made a conscious decision to stay away from it, after all I had enough negativity in my own head, I certainly didn't need anyone else's.

The harsh cold truth was now blindingly obvious.

We were *not* to be parents.

Our marriage was now a shadow of what it once was. Matt started taking overtime shifts three months earlier just to pay the bills. I'm sure he preferred to spend more time at work so he didn't have to be around me. We had now been trying to conceive for over five years. We had now spent over $30,000 and had nothing to show for it. I also needed to work to pay the bills, but I could think of nothing worse. I made an effort to go to school, but the sound of parents complaining about having to cook and clean for their ungrateful children was threatening to drive me completely mad. I began to feel angry and on more than one occasion I was dragged up to the new school principal's office to explain my inappropriate comments to parents. Jennifer West was a kind woman, but she certainly did not indulge or condone inappropriate behaviour from her teachers. She could not understand the change in me over the past twelve months and I just couldn't explain it to her either. It was all too much to bear.

Knowing when enough was enough was so difficult but I could not face another cycle. I could not face another disappointment. My hopes and dreams of being a mother had been shattered and I didn't know what else there was for me. My whole sense of self, my whole identity was tied up with being what I had always known I was going to be, a mother.

If I can't be a mother, then what am I? Who am I? What is my purpose? As I pondered this over the next weeks with a heavy and sad heart, my sister Melissa paid me an unexpected visit. She had spent the last seven years working in orphanages in India and Africa. And had made a flying visit home. I hadn't seen her for over three years. We had never been particularly close, and I really didn't know exactly what it was that she did in those orphanages; the only thing I did know was that her arrival on my doorstep obviously meant that she had been speaking to Mum. Her visit was short and sweet. I was in no mood to entertain Melissa, or to discuss my personal devastation with her. I couldn't discuss it with anyone let alone Melissa who would never understand. She could never understand. Melissa never liked children, never even wanted them. The fact that she was now working in orphanages was incredulous really and I had never taken the time to ask her why. Melissa played by a different set of rules. She was alternative, and nothing like me. She was always selfish and self-involved which is why what she did next came as such a shock.

Melissa and I sat and had a cup of tea, herbal for Melissa and black for me. We talked a lot about nothing in particular. We were like two strangers and I was not in the mood to be chatty, so after a suitably reasonable amount of time I cut the visit short saying I had a headache and needed to lie down. Melissa was catching a plane back to India that night, so I wouldn't see her again this visit, but I didn't care. I just needed to be alone. Melissa got up to leave and gave me a hug on the way out. It's funny, I really don't remember her ever hugging me before. I hardly remember her even being civil to me. It came as a bit of a shock, but I didn't give it any thought. As she said goodbye, she handed me an envelope saying, 'Open it later. Take care, Sarah', and she left.

I immediately opened the envelope as soon as Melissa drove away, more than likely not to be seen for another three years, and I couldn't believe my eyes. Inside the envelope was an open plane ticket to India. Anger instantly flooded through my body. *What the hell was she thinking? Why would I want to go to India? To spend time with a sister I don't even know at an orphanage filled with "children", the one thing I can't have? Does she just want to rub it in my face? This is so like her, over the top and so insensitive.* I screwed the ticket up and threw it as far as I could. It managed to slide across the wooden floor into the far corner of my office where it came to an unceremonious stop right under my desk, just out of sight.

Months pass slowly, Matt and I have been spending less and less time together, and I have to admit, it is more my fault than his. He has tried to be supportive, but I've been so horrible to live with. I can see it, but I just can't seem to do anything about it. I'm wracked with grief and guilt, but 'time waits for no man', as my dear departed grandfather would often say. *Why did I think I would be any different? Why did I waste so much precious time? What if I hadn't?* I can't help it, I ruminate over and over the same thoughts playing like a recording in my head I just can't turn off. I blame Matt some days, *he should have known we were waiting too long* and part of me knows that doesn't even make sense, but I think it anyway. I'm so angry and despairing that I just can't see any future for me without children. I can't understand why for some reason God has chosen me to be infertile. That terrible word. I never dared say out loud, but the truth is the truth.

I am infertile.

I'M INFERTILE.

I feel like screaming, but nothing comes out except for more tears. It's not bloody fair. I feel like a complete failure as a woman and nothing else matters, not school, not the house, not my career, not my family and not Matt. Even though I know all too well that I have a really poor prognosis and amidst all the despair and hopelessness, I am constantly plagued by one recurring thought: *What if I do just one more?*

CHAPTER 10
ONE MORE TRY

J ane popped by unexpectedly one Saturday Morning in late
January. Matt was away for a work conference, again. I had
been planning on spending the weekend in my pyjamas
watching TV. The sun was shining, and Jane had brought her
bathers in the hope that I had nothing planned and we could spend a
carefree day at the beach. The odds were somehow stacked in her
favour, as I spent most of my time at home now, venturing out only
when necessary. Matt had tried to entice me out with offers of
dinner or movies, but I always made an excuse. The fact was that
wherever I went all I saw was happy families, prams or pregnant
women. Staying home, although I couldn't really explain it to Matt,
was a far better option. I had been avoiding catching up with Jane
recently, actually I had been avoiding catching up with anyone.
When I thought about it I hadn't seen her since well before Christmas, perhaps early November. Christmas, the once joyous occasion
and all it entailed, was also now a time that I dreaded.

Jane was usually busy with her career and I was busy hiding from the world, but I could only hide from Jane for so long. She waltzed into my house, threw open the blinds and said with authority as she looked at me still in my pyjamas at eleven, 'Oh, good, you aren't doing anything today, we are going to the beach'. I noticed with dread that this was not a request. 'Grab your stuff. C'mon, Sarah move it'. Even saying I had a headache wouldn't fool her. She would always have some latest research to quote as to how salt water or sea air were thought to be beneficial for curing anything that ailed you, and so I reluctantly went to get changed.

We walked down to my favourite spot, threw down our towels and despite the fact I live only a few houses up the road, I realised that I hadn't been here since my last IVF cycle months ago. The weather was a perfect 28 degrees and the cloudless sky reflected onto the water to make the bay look the most stunning shade of blue that actually took my breath away. In that moment I wondered why I had stayed away for so long. *God, I have missed this place.*

'Come on,' Jane yelled, as she threw me the sunscreen and ran down to the water diving straight in.

I quickly applied the sunscreen, didn't wait the required ten minutes for absorption, and followed Jane to the water. The feeling of the cool water on my body was like an awakening. I felt alive for the first time in months. There is something so special, so sacred about the sea. It's as though it can wash away all my worries and concerns and leaves me feeling rejuvenated and invigorated. As we floated in the water looking at the sea bottom to discover who could find the best treasure the sea had to offer, I felt an overwhelming sense of gratitude to this beautiful friend who was bobbing around in the water with me. She knew me so well.

We spent hours at the beach that day laying on our towels reading and enjoying the warmth of the sun on our skin and cooling down in the crystal-clear water of the bay. There was no need for words. There was a comfort and familiarity we shared that said it all. Jane understood me, and I knew she was here for me today. I also knew that she would wait for me to talk when the time was right.

It was later in the evening over a glass of wine that I finally opened up to Jane about all that I had been experiencing over the last months. The total devastation that I had felt that was difficult for others to understand. I even discussed the endless thoughts in my mind that just wouldn't shut up about one more try.

'I just don't know what to do, Jane, all the money, all the heartache, but what if the next one is the one?' I said through welling tears.

I talked and talked until I could talk no more. It was as though I had opened a valve and everything I had been thinking and feeling just spilled out to this dear friend. Jane did not speak, she didn't offer platitudes or advice; she just listened. She just seemed to understand that I needed to talk. She did not judge me, and I didn't feel the need to have to justify what I was saying. Jane accepted me as I was.

When I was completely finished there was silence. As she poured us another glass of wine and said, 'I want to ask you just one question, Sarah.'

I looked at her and nodded acceptance.

'I don't want you to think about 'shoulds' or 'shouldn'ts' and I don't want you to think about anyone else, this question is all about you, Sarah. Actually, I don't want you to think at all, just take the very first thing that pops into your mind and answer me really quickly, okay?'

'Okay.'

'What do you need to do, Sarah, in order to let go of those repetitive thoughts and feel you have done enough?'

Without hesitation and without thought I quickly said, 'I need to do another cycle.'

Jane picked up her glass and clinked mine with a smile and said, 'Well there you go, Sarah. Decision made.'

My decision *was* made.

I really did need to do one more cycle.

When Matt came home from his conference, we sat out on our balcony, something we hadn't done together for a long time and I told him what I really needed to do. He hugged me and said that he was worried about me, but if that is what I wanted then that is what we will do.

The next day I made an appointment to see Professor Tom.

I was now thirty-seven, and the IVF clinic call this "advanced maternal age". As if I didn't feel bad enough, I was now being told by my specialist that because I was "advanced maternal age" there was a higher risk of genetic abnormalities. At thirty-seven I didn't feel "advanced maternal age". Women still have babies at thirty-seven but apparently this is the magic number after which things can really start to go pear-shaped. Fertility declines and genetic abnormalities become more common, not that I can say things have been smooth sailing up to this point. Embryo biopsy was an expensive option, in which they could screen embryos before implantation to exclude any abnormal embryos from transfer, but due to my embryo numbers and quality, this was probably not an option for us. To be honest, I was unsure how I felt about embryo biopsy, so I was glad the decision was made for us. The voices of the Sisters from St

Mary's School for good Catholic girls were still ringing in my ears, *if it is God's will it will be.* We were told that we could do antenatal screening, either a CVS or an amniocentesis to ensure the baby was fine during early pregnancy. At this stage I just wanted to get pregnant. We could explore all of those things later if by some miracle of God, I did get pregnant.

Professor Tom was going to try something different this time. I was going to do a cycle using a different drug that I hadn't been on before, something new called an "Antagonist".

An Antagonist, are you kidding me? Surely, he is joking, who would call a drug that? When it's about to be used on hormonal women? Someone with a death wish, perhaps.

But Professor Tom goes on to say that it will recruit the eggs in a different way. *Okay, recruiting is good, I'll try anything. Nothing else has worked, bring on the "Antagonist" and God help us all.* So, I prepare myself as best I can for our next IVF cycle. There is a part of me that dares to be hopeful, after all this is something different, and I just have a gut feeling that maybe this time ... but, I can't allow myself to get too confident, the fall is so devastating if things go wrong. Matt and I decide to wait a month and go with my next period. Delaying goes against all my instincts. Each month I wait I know my chances are reducing but by waiting, my blood tests, ultrasound appointments and theatre bookings will all fall in the next school holidays which means less overall stress for me. It is getting more and more difficult to have time off work, and pressure from school is an added tension that I just don't need. This will be my last cycle and I want everything to be perfect.

Over the next month, I take time to ensure my diet and physical health are as good as I can get them. I book in for several sessions of acupuncture after work and make an appointment to see my

Chinese herbalist. I even squeeze in a weekly massage ensuring I am at least physically at my best. All the while I try to keep my labile emotions in check as I mentally steel myself for what lies ahead.

Six weeks later my cycle begins.

The antagonist cycle is shorter, and soon enough it is time for my monitoring scans. Surprisingly the results on the day look hopeful. I wait for that call in the afternoon to see what I need to do next. Susan, my IVF lifeline and support person, is on a holiday and so I seem to just get bounced from one nurse to another. It feels a little like I'm in no-man's land, nobody seems to know my history and I am quietly annoyed at Susan for deserting me when I need her the most. Someone called Lisa eventually calls me and I'm booked for a repeat scan to check the follicles are growing at the right rate. To my relief they are, and theatre is scheduled three days later.

As I sit in recovery after my egg collection I feel relieved that I got three eggs, and I'm also slightly envious of the woman next to me who got thirty-five. I wonder how that is even possible. The nurses are concerned that she got too many and she may not be able to have her transfer this cycle. Now that's a problem I would like to have.

Three days later, the day of my transfer the embryologist tells me there are two little embryos still looking good and I choose to have both put back into my uterus. I was warned by a young nurse of the possibility of twins and a difficult pregnancy, and I once again felt annoyed that Susan was not with me. *Me, twins ... do these people even read my history?* I feel slightly irritated. I put the thoughts out of my mind. I was not going to let anything upset me today.

After the transfer I was given a request slip to have a pregnancy blood test two weeks later. Matt and I then left the IVF hospital for the last time ever to go home for the long and difficult wait.

I felt some breast tenderness three days before my blood test. Was I pregnant or was I getting my period? I couldn't tell. The wait was torture, so I decided against advice to do a urine test, it was negative. My heart sunk. *Why had I let myself dare to believe things would be different this time? Why hadn't I protected myself?* I was crushed. *That's it. It's all over.*

I went in for my blood test on the day scheduled with a heavy heart. I still didn't have my period, but I knew it was negative. I felt completely normal, so I braced myself for the inevitable and oh so familiar, bad news. Matt had gone to work. He offered to stay home and spend the day with me, but I insisted he go. I needed time to myself today. The call came at 2:50 on that Monday afternoon, it was Susan, she was back from her holiday and she sounded refreshed and chirpy.

'Hi Susan.' I said feeling fairly flat and hating the fact she was being so insensitive. 'It's okay, I already know it's negative.' I despondently said, just wanting the formalities to be over as quickly as possible.

'Full name and date of birth, Sarah.'

Again, I feel annoyed. *She knows it's me for God's sake.* I tell her, and she then goes on to say the words that shook my world.

'Congratulations, Sarah, you're pregnant, and the levels are great!'

Complete and utter disbelief overwhelm me.

'Sorry?' I said, trying to process what she said, but my mind stopped working. 'What did you say?'

Susan repeats my name and date of birth and tells me my HCG level is 137.

'Are you sure?' I ask in disbelief thinking there must be a mistake.

'I'm sure, Sarah. You are pregnant.'

The words I have longed to hear.

I start to cry, but this time the tears are tears of joy.

I can hardly speak as I incoherently try to thank Susan over and over. She laughs, and the sound of her voice lets me know she is genuinely pleased for me. We have been on this journey together from the start. She knows what I have been through and she sounds as happy as I am. She books me in for two more blood tests and a seven-week scan and tells me to make an appointment with Professor Tom for a few days after the scan. I can't take it all in, my head is spinning, I don't think I'm making much sense. I still can't believe it. I ask Susan to check again.

She giggles and just says, 'I'll send you a letter, it will all be in that. I think you had better hang up now, Sarah, and call Matt.'

Matt ... yes, Matt ... I need to tell Matt.

I didn't call Matt; this news could not be told over the phone.

I jumped into my car and drove to his clinic. Matt was in the tea room when I arrived, facing the sink. He turned around and saw me and a look of confusion came over his face. I smiled as tears of joy began to flow. I moved towards him with my arms extended and melted into his familiar embrace.

'Sarah?'

My face was buried into Matt's chest, but I managed to say the two words we had both longed to hear.

'We're pregnant!'

We stayed in that embrace for what seemed like hours. No words, for that moment it felt like the Matt and Sarah of old, almost as though the last five years didn't matter. When Matt finally pulled away to look into my eyes, I could see he had been crying too. Even though I was pregnant, I still couldn't quite let go of the feeling that this was too good to be true. Each time I had to call Susan for the results of my five and six-week pregnancy blood tests, my heart raced as I held my breath until I heard the comforting words, 'Sarah, your levels are going up normally'. Matt came with me for the seven-week scan. We both happily watched as we, for the first time ever, saw the tiny heartbeat of our now 7.2-week gestation baby.

We were ecstatic.

It was now real.

The little heart was beating at 130 beats per minute.

'Is that too fast?'

'No, they can beat a lot faster than that,' the sonographer replied.

He reassured us that everything looked fine. Something called the crown rump measurement was indicating that the foetus was only 6.6 weeks gestation, but we were told that small variation was perfectly normal. We left the clinic with a small photo of our baby and decided to go out to lunch to celebrate.

It was only now that we felt we could tell people that we were pregnant. The turmoil of past failed IVF attempts combined with having to deal with the expectations of family and friends who just didn't understand had over the years taken its toll. This time we decided to keep things to ourselves until we had something to tell.

Mother's Day which was fast approaching was a big event at the Johnston's. We all knew that it was really just another excuse for Mum to get all the family together. She loved having all her children and grandchildren around, and this year would be no different. 'The more the merrier' Mum would say. Over the last few years I had made myself scarce at such events, but this year was different. Mum was very happy to hear that we would be attending and naturally Jane would be there too. 'She's our adopted daughter', Mum would say almost joking but deep down we knew she was serious. Melissa was still in India, but Peter, Rick, Karen and Billy would all be there along with their respective partners and children. Matt's family and all the other in-laws were invited too. Some would come, some would not. It really didn't matter to Mum, as long as she had asked. I began to notice that for the first time in years I was looking forward to the family gathering and I enjoyed rediscovering that I really liked feeling this way. What a difference a few short months had made. A nearly forgotten, yet somehow so familiar, feeling of joy was overtaking my senses.

By Mother's Day I would be into the ninth week of my pregnancy, moving toward the second trimester. Everything had been going so well that Matt and I decided that we would choose this happy family occasion to tell everyone our wonderful news that we also were now having a baby.

The day of the gathering arrived, we told our parents first and they were all so happy for us. Matt's parents were overjoyed at the prospect of being grandparents for the first time. My mum was ecstatic and couldn't contain her joy. She, more than anyone, knew what I had gone through on this journey. She knew how much being a mother had meant to me, and she had prayed every day for me to find my peace throughout those long dark years of infertility.

I'm sure Dad wanted to lift me off the ground and swing me around as he always used to, but he thought better of it thankfully and was satisfied with a gentle hug and a heartfelt kiss on the cheek. 'Well done, Sarah, I'm so happy for you both,' he said in an emotional voice as tears were welling in his massive blue eyes. Then Big Johnno quickly turned away to wipe the welling tears as he moved toward Matt to give him a bear hug. 'Good onya Mate,' he said as he handed him a stubbie, 'Congratulations, about bloody time'. The remainder of the day was a delightful blur. We told the rest of the family our news and I felt the weight of the last five and a half years lifting. I was acutely aware of the tiny life growing within me and finally I felt as though I could breathe easily.

We did it.

CHAPTER 11
THE PREGNANCY

My pregnancy continued on delightfully and uneventfully despite the undercurrent of irrational thoughts that kept reminding me that something could still go wrong.

I chose to keep seeing my IVF specialist for ongoing pregnancy care. Professor Tom was also an obstetrician and gynaecologist and I felt comfortable that he knew my history and would take good care of me. At almost every visit there seemed to be a blood test, urine test or a scan to attend for this or that, so I felt confident that Professor Tom had it all covered.

Early in the pregnancy he had spoken to us about the possibility of antenatal screening. I quickly remembered with a sinking feeling in my stomach the whole "advanced maternal age" thing. Our choices were that we could have a CVS which was an early screening test at around eleven weeks or we could wait until later in the pregnancy and have an amniocentesis, which came with less risk of miscarriage. We were advised to think carefully about what we would do if the results were abnormal, but this was something I did not want to think carefully about at all, so I avoided the topic whenever Matt brought it up. I chose to keep my nagging feelings of doubt to myself. It was better this way. It was as if I believed that if I did not speak the words out loud they would cease to exist. We chose the amniocentesis option that could be done around the seventeen weeks gestation stage because we definitely didn't want any additional risk.

The procedure went very smoothly. Finally, everything seemed to be going our way. I continued on happily for the next two and a half weeks until we were due to see Professor Tom for the results. I didn't give any thought to what may or may not show up on the results during this long wait. I had been through long waits before. I truly believed that if God had allowed me to finally become pregnant after such devastating years of infertility, how could my little baby be anything else but normal?

Over these months of early pregnancy Matt and I began to rekindle our damaged relationship bit by bit, but we still had a long way to go. Things were different now, not so carefree as they once were. The intimate side of our relationship had suffered greatly and now that I was pregnant I didn't feel like making love anymore, even though Matt did. This was becoming yet another issue in our now fragile relationship. I knew that I was being irrational. Professor Tom had told us it was fine to have sex whenever Matt asked him the question, but it had now taken me nearly six years to get to this point and I was not going to allow anything or anyone to jeopardise my growing baby.

I had been looking forward to my nineteen-week scan which we had at the IVF clinic the day before our return visit to see Professor Tom. We should have had it the week prior, but Matt was interstate at a workshop and couldn't make it and so we waited. Matt was not wanting to miss out on anything to do with the pregnancy now, and I have to confess, there was a comfort having him by my side.

During the scan Matt and I finally got a glimpse of our baby. The sight of tiny limbs moving about filled my heart with joy. I could tell there were two arms and two legs but not much else. The swirling images of all shades of grey could have been a baby alpaca for all I could tell. I had to wonder as we both sat staring at that screen, how on earth anyone makes sense of this grey blur, but fortunately that was something I didn't have to worry about. The fact was someone *was* able to make sense of it and we were in good hands.

'Is everything all right?' I nervously asked the sonographer who was intently searching for tiny details amidst the swirling sea of grey images.

He didn't seem very excited about his amazing job of viewing new growing life. I suppose even the most exciting of things can become a bit ho-hum when you are doing them day in and day out. He pointed out the heart beating and the arms and legs, but he said he wasn't able to say too much about the details. Our doctor would give us the full report. He asked when we were seeing him.

'Tomorrow.'

'Excellent, I'll make sure he has the report first thing in the morning.'

And that was that.

The next day we were to get the full results of the scan and the amniocentesis. The thought scared me and excited me all at the same time. I allowed myself the luxury of imagining what this tiny little person growing inside of me looked like. I could now feel the gentle movements of life within me. At first, I was uncertain if I was imagining it, but now I was sure. The movements are stronger now and I may well have a little AFL footballer developing in there.

My belly was growing so much now and even though I was only nineteen weeks pregnant I was sure I looked at least eight months. There was something quite reassuring about this. My baby was growing, this must be a good sign, but even though the nagging thoughts and the *what ifs* were a little less frequent these days, I could always find them easily if I looked for them. I tried not to think about what could go wrong and instead focused my attention on the nursery. It was time to get painting.

The thought of being a dad was steadily growing on Matt. He was sure it was a boy and he was also sure our champion footballer would probably play footy for Hawthorn. 'We'll have to talk about that', I would say with a giggle. This thought always brought a smile to my face. I loved to see Matt dreaming about parenthood and all it entailed. He'll be a great father.

The sun was shining on that Thursday afternoon in late July when we made our way to the 4 pm appointment at Professor Tom's rooms. I was now nineteen and a half weeks pregnant and growing bigger every day, it seemed. I had physically been feeling wonderful during the pregnancy. Unlike my conception, everything had really gone to plan and had been very uneventful.

Professor Tom was seated behind his desk. He didn't seem his usual self.

'Hi, Sarah,' he nodded and gestured for me to sit down as he held out his hand to shake Matt's hand, 'Matt. Have a seat, I have the results of your tests.'

He looked me in the eyes and I instantly knew.

'I'm afraid it is not good news,' he continued.

Immediately an overwhelming wave of nausea floods through my body and I feel like I'm about to faint. I look at Matt in complete horror, he stares back at me with a mask of shock and sadness on his face.

'Just listen, Sarah,' he said in a monotone voice as he took my hand.

I hardly feel his hand in mine, it's as though my body is not my own. I turn back to Professor Tom. I open my mouth to try to speak but no words come out. Professor Tom goes on to say that the amniocentesis and our ultrasound scan both confirm that our baby has a genetic abnormality: Edwards Syndrome.

He continued on in the sincerest voice, 'I am so very sorry.'

He briefly explained that our baby had heart defects, oesophageal defects, kidney defects and brain defects, something called micro-cephaly which meant a very small head.

The words made no sense. I hardly heard anything after the word "abnormality". I could see Professor Tom's mouth moving. I knew he was talking but it was as if I had shut down and could not comprehend what he was saying.

'Sarah,' he said with a firm voice as he tried to get my attention. I stared at him as he said the words. 'Your baby's defects are so severe they are not compatible with life.' He took a deep breath and said with certainty just in case it was not already clear. 'Your baby will not survive.'

My head spun, and his words could hardly be heard over my own voice screaming in my head, *NOOOOOOOOOOOOOO, this can't be ... NO GOD, PLEASE!*

'The results are wrong,' I managed to say through a hoarse voice that sounded like it belonged to someone else. 'I'm so big. My baby is growing.'

Professor Tom explains in the gentlest of voices that polyhydramnios is part of the syndrome.

'There's too much amniotic fluid, Sarah,' he replied.

The syndrome ... the syndrome ... the harsh sound of the word "syndrome" rings in my ears and hits me so hard I feel like I've just been punched and winded.

I can't breathe.

I feel sick.

My baby has a syndrome? I need to get out of here, I need to run away from this place. I stand to leave but my legs don't want to carry me. I somehow manage to stagger to the door feeling completely betrayed by my body. I stumble into the waiting room, blinded by the tears in my eyes and manage to get to the bathroom. I enter the stall, collapse on the floor and vomit into the toilet.

Now the problem of waiting for the safer screening test instead of the one that you could have had done six weeks earlier is that you have another six weeks to get used to the idea of being pregnant. You have another six weeks to bond to a tiny life growing inside you. You have another six weeks to dream of being a mother and wonder what your baby will be like. During this extra six weeks you somehow manage to convince yourself that all is well because your uterus is getting bigger and bigger every day and because of that you also manage to convince yourself that the nagging feeling, which is telling you that something is wrong with your baby, is all just normal pregnancy anxiety.

Matt deals with the formalities and we leave the doctor's clinic that Thursday afternoon. Matt drives us home, not a word is spoken. We sit in stunned silence. Matt seems lost in his own thoughts and I feel completely numb. The silence is a blessing, it allows me avoidance of the inevitable conversation to come.

I don't want to talk.

I don't want to think.

We get home, Matt tries to speak to me about the "arrangements", but I have no words.

I go to the cupboard and pour myself a big glass of red wine, the first in eight months, I skull it quickly and go to bed.

The next day I open my eyes, and for one brief precious moment I forget what happened yesterday. Regretfully this moment passes quickly, and the inevitability of our situation crashes in on me like a heavy weight once again. Matt brings me a cup of tea and puts it on my bedside table and sits next to me.

I don't move.

'The rooms are calling today to make the arrangements,' he says.

Silence

'It's a boy, Sarah,' he whispers.

Silence.

I can't even look at him.

I was angry.

How could he talk about arrangements?

'Fuck the arrangements,' I said as I roll away from him. 'I'm not doing it. They can't make me do it, this is my BABY!' I scream.

Matt says nothing, he leans in to kiss me on the head and leaves the room. An hour later the phone rings. I pull the covers over my head and ignore what might be happening in the other room. I'm still in bed, it's eleven. I have nothing to get up for. Matt called the school and told them I would not be in for the next week. He brings me in another cup of tea. The other one is still on the bedside table untouched.

'We have been booked in to the hospital labour ward on Monday morning, Sarah,' he said. This time he doesn't wait for a reply, he turns and leaves the room.

We were scheduled to have an induced labour Monday to deliver my precious baby boy, long before he should ever have entered this world. My body felt cold. *Was it possible to pass out while you were lying down?* I wondered. Nothing was doing what I needed it to do, my body had betrayed me once again.

For the next three days we just went through the motions. My induction was booked for 9 on Monday morning. Apparently, they don't do them on the weekend, something about not enough staff. This all seems so natural to them, business as usual. The next three days were filled with tears and silence. Matt tried to comfort me as much as he could, but nothing mattered.

On Sunday evening he tried to hug me, but I pulled away. I didn't want his comfort, I wanted my baby.

'Everything will be all right, Sarah,' he said.

I screamed at him, 'SHUT THE FUCK UP! I'M NOT OKAY!

YOU'RE NOT OKAY! OUR BABY IS NOT OKAY! NOTHING IS EVER GOING TO BE OKAY AGAIN!'

I screamed so loudly and hysterically for what seemed like hours. I don't even know what was coming out of my mouth, but I was on a roll. Years of pent-up pain and emotion seemed to spill out of my mouth like a toxic volcanic explosion. I think I said some pretty hurtful things, because Matt just looked shocked. He stared at me as my tirade went on and on and on.

He said nothing at all.

When I had finished my vile attack, he simply turned and walked out the door without a word. Our relationship had now hit rock bottom. I would not have been surprised if he never came back, but four hours later he quietly slipped into the bed behind me and held me tenderly all night without saying a word. I could feel the gentle quaking of his body as he softly sobbed throughout the night. I don't think that either of us slept that night.

Morning came as it always does. *How was I going to get through today?* Matt had told my family and Jane, but I could not speak to anyone. Not even Mum. We are usually so close, but I just couldn't stand to speak to anyone. There was too much sadness. I didn't want to be social. I struggled to even get out of bed the last three days.

Matt opens the blinds. I ask him to shut them again. Just make it still be night, I don't want it to be morning yet. I just wanted a little more time with my baby boy. This beautiful life growing inside of me. How was I going to willingly put an end to the pregnancy? The pregnancy I prayed for and worked so hard to get. The pregnancy that took nearly six years to achieve. I deserved this baby, Matt deserved this baby. Perhaps, they were wrong.

Tests are wrong sometimes. I can feel him moving inside of me. How do they expect me to kill my baby! I won't do it, I can't do it. I tell Matt to call the labour ward and cancel the induction.

'I'm not going through with it. I'll have the baby, and we'll take our chances.'

Matt wisely says a quiet 'okay'. I want to run away and keep my precious baby safe, but my legs are still. I pull the blankets over my head and cry some more. I'm not sure if it is possible to become dehydrated from crying, but if it is, I must be getting close. I never knew it was even possible to cry so much. The pain of nearly six years of treatments, financial concerns, disintegration of our sex life and ultimately our relationship, injections, scans, blood tests, more investigations, doctor visits, theatre procedures, acupuncture, herbal treatments, embryo transfers, failed fertilisation, cancelled cycles and failure after failure after failure after failure had all culminated in this moment. My body felt heavy and my heart felt even heavier. *I may never get out of this bed again. Please God, let me sleep and wake up and find that this was all a terrible dream.* But it was not a terrible dream.

Eventually and regrettably I leave the house that morning and as I do, I pass the room that was to be the nursery and stop to look in. All the hopes and dreams that we had for that room were now gone. The room feels cold. I look at the soft teddy bear that has sat in that corner since Matt brought it home the day after our seven-week scan. 'Our baby needs a birth teddy', he had happily said. I walk into the room and I pick up birth teddy and hand it to Matt. 'We need to take this', I say, 'Our baby needs a birth teddy.'

We arrive at the hospital and walk to the delivery suite and we are greeted by the midwife who will be with us today. She was expecting us; her name is Jenny. She greets us and ushers us towards a private room. The sounds of a woman in labour down the hall and a crying baby from another direction assault my senses. We pass a room, door ajar and I glimpse a new mother adoringly staring into the eyes of her little bundle of joy. I feel completely numb.

They begin my induction. I have something called Prostin Gel inserted to get my body ready. A few hours later a drip is put into my arm to start my labour and at 4:35 on that Monday afternoon the 3rd day of August 1998, our beautiful baby boy was born motionless.

We call him George.

His little hands were clenched, and his little legs were crossed. The midwives covered his tiny little head and body in a small soft blue blanket and handed him to me. He was not much bigger than the size of my hand.

I held him tenderly as I gently sobbed.

This little boy was mine and even with all his imperfections, he was perfect to me. Matt and I cried together as we sat with our baby for hours until we were finally ready to say goodbye. During this time there was a knock on our door and Jenny our midwife asked if I wanted to see my mother. I silently nodded. Matt had asked her to come against my wishes. I had told him that I didn't want to see or speak to anyone. Mum entered the room without a word. She somehow understood that there were no words for this situation. She walked over to me, held out her arms and cradled my head deep into her chest and gently stroked my hair as she rocked me ever so slowly back and forth. The gentle movement comforted me like no words ever could.

I silently sobbed.

George was in his cot, birth teddy by his side.

Mum looked at our baby boy and simply said with complete sincerity, 'He is beautiful, Sarah.' She looked me in the eyes and said, 'You're a mother now my beautiful girl, and nothing can ever change that'. I really needed my mum at that moment. I was so grateful that she did not stay away.

CHAPTER 12
WHAT JUST HAPPENED TO ME?

Days pass in a complete blur over the next week. A somehow protective numbness was pressing down on me like a heavy weight. Matt and I hardly speak. I have no desire to talk and eventually he stops trying. I look at him sometimes when he is unaware of me staring at him and I wonder what will become of us. He seems completely drained. I think this is just about all he can cope with. The thought that our relationship may be over would normally terrify me but instead I feel nothing at all. Our wonderful marriage is now but a shell of what it once was, and my ongoing actions continue to destroy the last fragile threads that have persisted against the odds to hold us together. I don't even care, and I do nothing to prevent it. It seems I am on an unstoppable path of self-destruction.

I was officially now at my lowest ebb.

My life was not to be as I had always imagined.

How could this have happened to me and why? What did I do to deserve this? Why am I being punished? I'm nearly thirty-eight, "childless", *after a voluntary* "termination" *of a child that could never have lived.* Even the term makes me feel sick. *How could I do that? Who am I to do that?*

You terminate a subscription, or an interview, not a child. Part of me knows I am being irrational, but there is still this part of me that is filled with self-loathing, this must be my fault. *Will God ever forgive me?* Everything is such a mess, my marriage may as well be over, nothing seems fair, nothing seems to make sense anymore. I wanted everything to be perfect and now I'm filled with so many regrets. *I waited too long. Mum told me my clock was ticking. Why didn't I listen to her? Why?*

I spend my days wondering, what if, what if, and then there's the wasted money, tens of thousands of dollars and what is there to show for it? Nothing. Nothing but heartache and despair. We are in debt. We have re- mortgaged the house twice to cover the medical bills, not that any of that matters, we will have to sell it soon enough. Matt hates me, I hate me, I am horrible to be around. I have lost my friends, because I couldn't stand to be around their happy families. I have even alienated my own family because they just didn't understand what I was going through. I don't even care about my job anymore. The job that was once so important to me. The job that was my reason for waiting. The job that I worked so hard to get. I have had so much time off for doctor appointments, blood tests, not to mention all the "collapse on the floor and cry days" that my work are trying to discretely suggest perhaps I would be happier somewhere else. They are now officially as tired of me as I am of myself. I don't even have the energy anymore to get angry. I just feel numb. Most days I can't even seem to drag myself out of bed. Matt says, his friend Roger says, 'I'm depressed'. He Googled it. *FUCK Roger!* I scream inside my head unable to pull up the energy to scream out loud. *Roger with his perfect little fertile partner and his perfect little family. What the fuck does Roger know about anything?* I pull the covers over my head once again and try to shut out the world. *What the hell is a "Google" anyway? I'm going to quit my job. I have to get away from here.* I just can't look at these sad walls any longer that remind me of hopes and dreams that will now never be. Where could I go? What could I do?

I recall the plane ticket that Melissa gave me which now seems like a lifetime ago and I'm filled with regret that I threw it away—but, then I remember. I jump out of bed, go into my office and crawl under my desk and there to my absolute astonishment, in the far corner where it has laid untouched out of sight and out of mind for all those long months, is the discarded crumpled open travel ticket.

I call the school and quit my job, effective immediately. This is completely unprofessional of me, and so out of character, but it feels good. It's the first thing that has felt good in a long time. I get no argument from "the vulture" when she takes my call, although I think I detect a slight sadness in her voice. 'We wish you all the best. Sarah', she says. I quickly disregard her comments as I think about how smug Melissa will be when I arrive.

God, I hate her right now, but anywhere has to be better than this.

PART II
NEW BEGINNINGS

CHAPTER 13
INDIA

I sit in the plane lost in thought. I am exhausted from lack of sleep and still my body refuses to yield. The random and constant thoughts in my head keep me awake. I have never been to India before, never even flown anywhere on my own. I can't even comprehend what awaits me in this foreign country. Mum dropped me off at the airport with a sad but hopeful look on her face as she said, 'I'm going to miss you so much my darling girl, but I think this will be good for you Sarah'.

Matt and I are now officially finished.

There's a part of me that still loves and cares for him. It is strange to think of him with someone else, but there's a numbness inside of me now that keeps those thoughts at bay as I think of my future without him. I truly hope he finds someone with whom he can have children, so he can finally be the father he so deserves to be. There is another part of me that is heartbroken at the thought, but I know it is for the best. I am aware I am running away but I can do little else. It's as though my mind is not my own anymore, the sensible and level-headed Sarah has deserted me, and I don't know if she will ever come back. I have left Matt to deal with the mess of selling our house and dividing our possessions. I have no care about any of it at the moment. I trust him and know he will do the right thing.

Melissa is meeting me at the airport and I feel a strange sense of connection with her now that has been missing from our relationship for what seems to have been my entire life. She was happy that I had decided to come, and she has arranged everything. She seems somehow different, I can't quite put my finger on why or how, but I sense a compassion from her that has surprised me.

It is early September when I touch down on Indian soil. As I make my way into the terminal I spot Melissa in the crowd of onlookers. She looks tanned and not at all out of place in this strange environment in which I find myself. She greets me with a welcoming heartfelt embrace and then quickly says, 'How was your flight?' Without waiting for an answer, she turns and says, 'Let's get your bags and get out of here'.

Even though it is 8pm local time as I make my way out of the hustle and bustle that is Delhi Airport, I am immediately struck by the heat and humidity that engulfs me. I follow Melissa who skilfully navigates her way through the throngs of people that appear to be fifty-deep in every direction, to our awaiting and very aged mini bus which has been borrowed from the orphanage to facilitate our journey.

Melissa throws my bags in the back and says, 'Jump in we've got a long drive'. The roads and drivers are even more of a shock to my senses as there seems to be no rules at all. Horns honk and what appears to be a "move first, think later" attitude applies that creates a feeling of tension in me to the point that I have to close my eyes several times to avoid seeing the inevitable collision that surprisingly never happens. Melissa notices the look of shock and trepidation on my face and laughs. She tells me I'll get used to it. 'We have a three-hour drive ahead of us back to the orphanage', she says, 'you had better relax'.

I begin to realise that I actually know surprisingly little about where I am going and what I'm about to experience. I have never been so spontaneous in my entire life. My decision to pack a bag and leave my life behind is so out of character for me I have to wonder if I am going completely insane. My usual considered and well thought out decisions have always served me well. I feel a small twinge of anxiety about the unknown that lies ahead as I begin to wonder if this was a good choice.

My mind slips back to my precious little baby George, and I start to feel the old familiar heavy weight of despair pressing down on me once again. I try not to think about it all and redirect my attention to the open window that apparently serves as the only air-conditioning in this incredibly hot place. As I continue to look out the open window of the mini bus, the smells, sounds and sights of this city awaken my senses and for a while I say nothing. Melissa strangely somehow seems to understand and allows me to sit in silence for as long as I need.

There is a smell of incense in the air. Melissa says it is burnt everywhere here. She tells me that people light it to attract Lakshmi, the Goddess of Wealth and Prosperity, into their houses, but just quietly I think it is more to hide the other less pleasant stench that permeates the air and to the uninitiated seems to be a kind of cross between the smell of putrid rubbish and urine. This odour is combined with the slightly more aromatic yet equally as prominent smell of fresh spices arising from the houses and roadside stalls.

As we drive I notice that people are cooking everywhere on roadside carts and even at this time of night the streets are alive with activity. The Indian people stare at me as I stare back with wide eyes and a look of astonishment on my face that anywhere else would have felt extremely rude, but here as I am struck by what I see, I can't stop myself from staring at everyone and everything. This is certainly nowhere like I have ever been before. I settle in for the long haul to the orphanage.

Although the mini bus was surprisingly comfortable, the torn but carefully mended seats told their own story. A story of poverty combined with a respectful kind of dignity that I find somehow comforting. In this country it was clear that things were not so easily discarded. I felt a slight pang of guilt as I thought of some of the things that I had discarded recently. Things that these people probably never even dare to dream about, things that we, in Australia, take for granted.

My mind goes to Matt and I feel a great sense of sadness. I brush away the tears that come and return my gaze to the open window. I am again struck by the intense heat that even at this time of night touches my skin as I once again inhale the pungent smells of this country. I see people living in shanties near the roadside and I am beginning to get a real sense of the poverty that exists here, and all the while our little mini bus continues on against all reasonable odds to ramble along the unmade roads toward our destination, the "Bacce' Asha Orphanage". Melissa says it means Children of Hope, in Hindi.

An hour into our journey Melissa breaks the silence and asks about Mum and Dad. Mum dropped me off at the airport, she's fine and Dad is Dad, no surprises there but he is looking old now. Silence falls again as I reflect on those words. Mum is still and always has been my inspiration and at sixty-eight years of age she is still incredible. If ever I ask how she is, she defiantly tells me she has no time to be unwell. Her determined voice rings in my ears: *I just won't have it, Sarah, you are only as old as you feel.* I'm not quite sure if that is true, but if it is then I must be about ninety-seven years old right about now.

I'm very aware of the silence which at any other time would have felt awkward, but I have no desire to make polite conversation right now and I really don't care if I am being rude. Melissa doesn't seem to mind, she is happy to sit with the silence, but further down the road she asks how Mum is dealing with retirement. She and I both know how important Mum's work was to her. I have to laugh at the thought of Mum retired.

'You do know, Melissa, that Mum never actually retired, don't you? She just gave up getting paid.'

I think she is almost busier now than she was before. She was always able to juggle so much; a huge family with all the dynamics and work. It is fairly astounding when I think about everything she seamlessly managed so confidently that most of us didn't even know what she was achieving. It's funny how that works, we always noticed if something was not done, but I'm not really sure we all appreciated just what was being done. Mum was always a *coper* and still is. Now, she no longer works as a senior clinical nurse specialist on the children's ward at the hospital; however, she has for the last three years been president of the Hospital Social Committee which raises funds for much needed equipment. She jokingly says in true Johnston style that they weren't getting rid of her that easily.

Mum loves life, loves family and loves to be involved. I think it was really hard for her to finally retire three years ago when she turned sixty-five, but she has definitely filled her time with so many things that keep her active and involved. She volunteers at the local special needs school once a week and helps out with the reading programme and looks after Karen's latest little bundle of joy on a Wednesday, so Karen can get to work.

Karen, now a mother of three, says work is a bit of a break from the constancy of parenting. As I think of this I feel a sudden jolt of jealousy combined with an uncontrollable feeling of anger shooting through me as I wonder how it is that the ever-so-fertile Karen can so easily leave her children to have a break! Perhaps, if she had any idea just how blessed she is she may choose to think otherwise. Thoughts like these and so many others have almost been feeding the dark feelings I have been experiencing over the last month. Hell, who was I kidding? More like over the last *years* and I notice that they are beginning to weigh me down once again. I feel an anger descending and I make a conscious choice to look back out the window and breathe. My psychologist told me I need to just breathe. Anger surges again. *What the hell does she think I've been doing all this time. Surely, she can see I'm not dead yet!*

Melissa points out a temple as we drive passed it, and I remember when Mum and Dad went to Bali—it was for their twentieth wedding anniversary—the one and only time I remember them ever having a holiday alone. Uncle Sid moved in for ten days to look after us, and the Johnston household was never the same again.

'Do you remember when Mum and Dad went to Bali?' I ask Melissa in a kind of monotone emotionless voice.

She just gave me a "look" that said it all and began to giggle. I gave her a slight smirk back as I tried to maintain my rage, but as hard as I tried, I couldn't stop myself beginning to giggle too. I thought about all that we had to endure for months and months after they returned as Dad constantly recounted every moment in excruciating detail. I looked at Melissa's amused face and I knew she was thinking exactly the same as I was, and it was then as if a pressure valve released and I started to laugh. Not just a little laugh, a real belly laugh, that once I started I couldn't stop. Melissa laughed at me laughing and in that moment, I forgot the last few years. It was the first time I had really laughed in a very long time and it felt good.

'Remember the photo presentation night,' Melissa said.

More laughter, I could hardly speak now.

I looked out the window as I remembered. Two weeks after Mum and Dad returned from Bali and after ten rolls of film came back from Kodak processing we all had to gather on a cold Melbourne winter's evening, Uncle Sid included, and endure a two-hour presentation from Dad of all the holiday shots. One whole roll was over exposed, and another roll had a misplaced finger in front of the lens that obstructed the view of a full twenty-four shots, but Dad still made us look at them all as he excitedly attempted to describe what was hiding behind the offending finger. Peter in a vain attempt to avoid the torture pretended he was sick, but Dad, not wanting Peter to miss out, gave him his own private viewing on the Sunday night about the time that Peter's favourite TV show was on. The rest of us walked past the door of the lounge and pulled faces at him when Dad couldn't see us, it was family fun at its best. Peter who always flew just under the radar to avoid such unpleasantries finally got caught out.

I settled back for the remainder of the drive in silence. The laughter had left me feeling a strange sensation in the pit of my stomach and my chest, a kind of comfort that I had not felt in a long time. My thoughts again went to Matt and our beautiful cottage by the sea, where we had often spent our evenings on the balcony laughing and sharing our days. Those times seemed so long ago now, and I am suddenly struck by just how happily naïve I was back then, and I wondered if I would ever be that carefree again.

As our little mini-bus continued to rattle and shake its way along the made roads of the larger towns I was struck by the people I saw bedding down by the road side. Melissa aware of my stunned stare tells me that there are over 250,000 children living on the streets of India. They have no schooling, most have no idea of right or wrong, they just have to somehow survive. They have been abused and taken advantage of in every kind of way. Most have never had a chance.

'We have had a very privileged life, Sarah.'

I sit quietly and feel the heaviness of the injustice and the hopelessness of all I am viewing coming in around me.

'This is why I'm here, Sarah,' Melissa whispers.

Her emotion is almost palpable, and I finally begin to get a glimpse of the real Melissa, a sister I have never really known or understood. A woman, it seems, of unexpected caring, and I wonder why it is that I have never seen this side of her before. We live in a world where so few have so much and so many have literally nothing. Perhaps it was the exhaustion from lack of sleep and long hours of travel that when combined were causing me to have this deep sense of profound reflection.

It was now 11:40 p.m. local time as we reached the orphanage. I notice a small poorly-lit sign out the front of a clay coloured wall. I'm not really sure what the wall is made of, but it looks like mud clay and it seems to surround the entire orphanage. The sign which proudly states this place is the Bacce` क Asha Orphanage: Children of Hope Orphanage, and "All Children are Welcome Here" hangs just next to a large gate that is locked. Melissa stops and unlocks the gate to allow us entry to a dirt courtyard area where the bus is parked, and the gate is locked behind us.

'Just a precaution', she says, smiling. 'I'll show you to your room for tonight and tomorrow we'll get you settled in.'

I'm shown to a small room, barely big enough for a single bed and a small bedside table. It reminds me of the tiny rooms the nuns used to have at the school convent. I instinctively look for the cross above the bed but find instead a small framed, slightly faded picture of the Dalai Lama.

'It's small, but it's private,' Melissa says. 'You'll be able to get some sleep tonight and I'll wake you at 6:15 for breakfast.'

'6:15!' I exclaim.

'Yes, thought I'd give you a sleep in on your first day. Enjoy it because it probably won't happen again, usually we rise at five in the morning, wash and clean up and meet at 5:30 in the hall for morning meditation followed by morning exercise, it's the best part of the day,' she says, as she leaves me to get ready for bed.

My mind immediately goes to the memory of Melissa spending whole weekends in bed and refusing to get up even on school days. Surely this is not the same Melissa. I want to ask her who she is and what has she done with my sister, but instead I put my bag down and make my way to the communal bathroom down the hall.

The bathroom is old but very clean with white painted walls and a tiled floor. On one side are several small cubicles containing western style toilets and on the other side more cubicles containing showers. There's a central sink area that is more like several large troughs for washing in. I quickly do what I need to do and make my way back to my room. I sit on the surprisingly comfortable bed in my tiny, yet private room and look around. I'm overcome with a feeling of weariness and it makes me feel like crying. The sense of the unknown is closing in on me and I am again questioning if I should have come here at all. I hear the words of my mother sounding in my ears *nothing good ever comes from thinking after 9 o'clock Sarah, just go to sleep.* I consciously try to shut out the thoughts and remember to breathe, my psychologist would be proud. Just for a moment, I lay on the bed fully clothed, but exhaustion finally wins as I fall asleep.

I awaken to the sounds of activity outside my room as I realise I have slept the entire night in my clothes. I'm still exhausted, but there will be no more sleeping this morning it seems. I look at my watch and notice it is 6:10. A few minutes later there is a knock at the door. It's Melissa.

'Oh, good, you're up, how'd you sleep?'

'Like a log.

'Great, do you need to wash up? Breakfast is in the main hall at 6:30. Just follow the kids, you'll find it, I'll see you there.'

As I look around I once again wonder what I am doing here, this place is so foreign, but as my mind automatically goes to the mess I have left behind I realise with a tinge of sadness that I really have nowhere else to be and nothing to go back to. I make a decision to give this strange place a chance, after all, how bad can it be? I steady myself in my little room gathering the courage to open the door and face whatever it is the day has in store for me, and as I do, I experience the strangest sensation. It's a mix of anxiety somehow combined with sadness because I instinctively know that when I open that door I will be taking the first steps in my new life: a

SARAH'S STORY LIFE AFTER IVF

different life, a life without Matt, a life without children. The irony strikes me as I take a breath and bravely open the door and find myself in a corridor surrounded by children of all ages scurrying past me from the bathroom as they make their way to the communal dining area for breakfast.

Well here goes. The sight of the children once again reminding me of all that I have lost, but today, I cannot allow those thoughts, or I know I will stop functioning. I block them out and go to the bathroom and then as instructed follow the stream of children to the dining area.

The food hall is large and bustling with excited children interspersed with what would seem to be Caucasian helpers. The room is sparsely furnished with long wooden tables and bench seats, which are the main feature. I'm struck by the simplicity of this place. There is nothing unnecessary here. To my surprise I notice a few Buddhist monks in robes sitting silently at the corner table, they seem to be in silent prayer.

I spot Melissa and she directs me to a place on a table with some of the other helpers. 'I'm on breakfast', she says to me 'so I can't sit with you today, but this is David and Stephanie, they will fill you in on the day's routine'. Metal bowls are placed before us and a large metal pot and ladle is positioned on all the tables. A chime sounds and the hall falls silent. As a teacher I am used to dealing with children; however, I am somewhat astounded at the sudden and respectful stillness that fills the hall as a morning blessing for the food is given by a young monk. After the blessing, the morning meal that looks like a kind of oat porridge is ladled out into the bowls by a helper strategically positioned on each table to assist and supervise the children.

I had not given much thought to the origins of this place but over breakfast David and Stephanie give me a quick rundown. Apparently, some of the older monks here escaped from Tibet to India during the Chinese invasion of 1950. Lama Ngawan, the head monk here and Maha-Thera Sonam are now the only two remaining of the original group of monks who made this journey. Together, and with others, they travelled until they found this place and established a sanctuary in which to care for and educate orphans and displaced children.

Stephanie who is from England tells me with a cheeky grin, 'He doesn't talk much.' She giggles as she gesticulates to Lama Ngawan.

'Funny, you know, his name means teacher of powerful speech,' Stephanie adds. 'One of life's mysteries, Stephanie.' David says as they gather the bowls and leave the table.

I look over to the place Lama Ngawan is seated, he has a certain air about him, a presence that I find intriguing. My eyes meet his gaze and I feel as though he can see right through me. I quickly look away feeling slightly embarrassed that I was caught staring and make my way into the kitchen with the bowls.

I spot Melissa with her back toward me at a large sink area on the far wall. To the right is the cooking area, there are cooktops covered in large pots, some with aromatic spices simmering and bubbling away, probably for lunch or dinner, others with the remnants of the morning meal. To the left there are more benches and storage shelves above and below a smaller bench. Again, I am aware of the function and simplicity of the area. Everything has a place and a purpose. Nothing unnecessary. Melissa turns and takes the bowls from my hands and goes back to the washing up. 'Grab a towel, Sarah, and start drying, there is plenty more where they came from', she gestures to the bowls still in need of washing. 'When you have dried them, stack them there', she points to the large extensive wooden central bench that appears to be for food preparation but at the moment is covered in the returned breakfast pots and bowls. I clear a spot and begin stacking the clean dishes on the cleared bench and for a while I am so engrossed in my chore that for a moment at least I can forget the world.

When breakfast is finished, Melissa gives me a tour of the orphanage and the existing buildings. There are several large halls and rooms off a central courtyard that serve as multipurpose areas. Some for dining, some for schooling, some for prayer and meditation. The sleeping dormitories are positioned all together to one side. Within the courtyard, which often serves as a space for morning exercise or quiet reflection, is a stone sculptured sitting Buddha who appears to preside over all the activities therein. There is a real sense of serenity within this space and I have to wonder if it was facilitated by the sight of a reflective monk sitting in quiet meditation to my left. I wasn't sure, but there was certainly a tangible feeling here that was comforting. I felt compelled to want to spend some time here and hoped that this much needed tranquillity would permeate through me too.

Melissa explained how everyone here had a part to play in the running of this place. Everyone had their job and other chores such as kitchen, laundry, and cleaning were shared.

'I have put you down to assist with the teaching of the children, given your expertise I thought it was a good fit,' Melissa said.

I felt a sudden surge of anxiety that somehow quickly morphed into anger and began to flood through my body. It seemed uncontrollable as my mind immediately went to my precious little George. I could no more teach children right now, than I could scale Mount Everest without climbing gear and oxygen equipment. My face must have paled because Melissa suddenly looked concerned and asked me if I needed to sit down. *What the hell was I doing? Why had I come to this place?* This place and these children that were a constant reminder of my own failures.

'I can't do it, Melissa,' I finally manage to get out. 'I just can't do it.'

As anger turned to the deepest sadness within me the tears I had been holding back began to flow freely and for a while I didn't care. Melissa seemed to be comfortable enough to just let me cry. She guided me to a nearby stool and just sat with me in silence and held my hand. She seemed to understand that I didn't want to speak. I eventually composed myself and as I did, through tear blurred eyes, I noticed Lama Ngawan observing me. His gaze directed towards me was undecipherable. In my emotional state I could not interpret if it was curiosity or perhaps love or compassion behind that gaze. Maybe it was pity, it was impossible for me to tell but it somehow unsettled me as I reflected on the scene later that day. This was a man unlike any other I had encountered, and even from afar I couldn't explain the compelling feeling growing within me to know more about him.

Melissa arranged for me to spend the next few days in the kitchen and laundry areas far away from the children. I avoided early morning meditation and exercise sessions by volunteering for the early breakfast shifts. It was a way of steering clear of the children and everything they represented, and it also kept me very busy. I could therefore avoid, at least for a while, the constant and oh, so, repetitive negative self-thoughts that had become my habits. So, for a while at least, I was blissfully existing in a temporary state of denial. I spent my spare time between designated chores strolling the grounds and exploring the area just outside the gates that surrounded the orphanage. As the weeks passed, I began to find time to sit with my sorrow, and grieve my little boy, who was never to live in this harsh world with me. I gained some small comfort from the fact that my precious baby would never know or experience such sorrow. He was forever innocent and the strongest maternal part of me was in some way grateful for that.

As the weeks rolled by, I found myself spending more time in the grounds just outside of the orphanage and as I did, I began to notice that Lama Ngawan also had a habit of spending quiet reflection time in the surrounding outdoor areas. I noticed his orange robes swishing past me on more than one occasion, always at a respectable distance and always with eyes averted to avoid any eye contact. I had *not* noticed if this curious monk ever spoke to the other volunteers, but from Stephanie's original comments, I thought he probably did not.

Over the weeks that followed my fascination for him grew stronger and as it did, I began to notice a certain pattern to his routines that intrigued me. He seemed to have a favourite spot, sitting on a perfectly shaped rock shelf on a slightly elevated hilltop to the north, that when correctly positioned, provided a person with the perfect vantage point from which to have a clear view of the entire orphanage. I too, found myself beginning to seek out this position to sit with my pain and sorrow. From time to time, despite my best efforts not to, I found myself lost in the antics of the children within the walls of the orphanage as they happily played almost without a care in the world, or so it seemed from afar.

I always ensured I arrived after Lama had left, his preferred time I established was early morning, I on the other hand made a habit of arriving after the midday meal was complete and my chores were done. On one occasion, nonetheless, as I sat with my thoughts staring at nothing in particular, I became aware of a familiar sound of the rustle of orange robes approaching and almost instantaneously I experienced a kind of guilty feeling such as a naughty child would experience when the teacher discovers them doing something forbidden. There was no way out, nowhere to go, I had been seen and I just had to wait and see what was about to happen. Lama Ngawan's approach slowed as I dared to glance nervously toward him, his eyes met mine and without a word or a decipherable expression he stopped and sat to my left about two metres away from me. The silence seemed deafening.

'Hello Lama, I'm sorry … would you like to be alone? I can leave.' I managed to say as I started to stand.

He simply raised one hand in a gesture to tell me there was no need for me to go, and so despite the fact that I was actually ready to leave, I decided to stay sitting with this intriguing man in silence for half an hour longer, at which time he stood and left me with nothing more than a respectful nod of his head. Feeling curious, I too, slowly made my way back to the orphanage ensuring I kept a respectable distance behind him.

Later that day, I spoke to Melissa about my interlude with Lama Ngawan. She seemed quite surprised.

'He generally keeps his distance from the new people. He doesn't talk much,' she said.

'Really?'

'Yeah, really,' she said with a giggle. 'You must be special, Sarah.'

I continued my afternoon visits to that particular spot for a few days in the hope that perhaps the Lama would return, but he did not. Not until five days later when he once again came and sat two metres to my left. After a brief respectful head nod to acknowledge my presence he again sat in silence.

'Lovely day,' I said, but to no avail.

It was apparent Lama was not going to speak. After ten minutes of silence, I had to leave as I was required in the kitchen for the evening preparations.

As I stood to leave Lama said, 'What do you see, Sarah?' Without averting his eyes from all he surveyed.

I was taken by surprise, I had not expected him to speak, but not only had he spoken, he knew my name.

'Nothing, I see the orphanage.'

I immediately regretted my answer. *Nothing! Why did I say nothing? God, I'm such a doofus!* I waited for what seemed like an eternity for him to speak again but he did not.

CHAPTER 14
FINDING SARAH

Life in the orphanage was consistent and ordered. In those first weeks the structure was a comfort to me. I knew where I was supposed to be and what I was supposed to be doing, nothing more, nothing less. This allowed me a certain freedom to completely immerse myself in the daily routines which in and of itself was a comfort. There was no need to think, no need to question, no need to feel. The anonymity I had here was a blessing too. I kept pretty much to myself as I had no desire to discuss my life. I had no need to talk about Matt, George or infertility. I'm not even sure if I realised at the time that I was existing in a somewhat unrealistic state of avoidance, but for those early weeks it somehow worked for me. I set about doing my chores to the best of my ability and I spent most of my free time alone. When solitude was not possible, Melissa, Stephanie and David were my companions. Stephanie and David seemed to respect my need for privacy without it ever having to be asked for. I'm sure that Melissa had filled them in on my story; *I was the foolish sad woman who made poor choices and had ruined everything she*

touched. Killer of an unborn child, destroyer of marriages, sinner in the eyes of God.

Yes, it was best not to think.

In those early weeks, I also did my best to avoid developing any relationships with the children, but as the weeks passed I found it more and more difficult to avoid. My natural love for children began to peep through the hardened veneer of sadness that I had wrapped around myself at the most inconvenient of times. Some of the children, perhaps sensing that part of the old Sarah that now for the most part remained hidden from public view, followed me around as though I was the pied piper.

'Miss Sarah, play with us,' one would say. 'Miss Sarah, where are you going? Miss Sarah, you're pretty.'

I worked hard to maintain my resolve to be unhappy. After all, if I did not maintain my sadness I was surely somehow disrespecting the life of my baby George. I was somehow disrespecting the life I was supposed to live as a wife and mother. The life that it was now apparent I would not live.

It was on one such day as I sat fully immersed in my sadness, reflecting on the unfairness of it all, that a child slipped, fell and cut his knee in front of me. There was blood beginning to flow as the young boy, who looked to be around ten years old, limped over to where I was sitting. He climbed onto my lap and hugged me. A single tear that had turned into a trail of muddy water on his face smeared into my shirt as he sought my comfort. 'It's okay,' I said to him, 'let's get this cleaned up'. I went to stand but was surprised to hear him say that he was fine. He was actually trying to comfort me; I apparently looked so sad that he thought I needed a hug. He told me that he always felt better when Melissa hugged him if he was sad and that Melissa was his family, and he was very lucky to live here. He proudly stated that he was blessed by Buddha.

I looked into this dirty, skinny, little boy's eyes and I felt so humbled. This child who has nothing, this child who has no one, wanted to make *me* feel better. His name was Raaj.

Day by day chinks began developing in my armour as I started spending more time in the children's area. Initially this was more their doing than my own and possibly mostly due to the persistence and insistence of that same particular young Indian boy, Raaj. After many rejections and when he could no longer accept my polite avoidance he reached out and gently took me by the hand and directed me to sit.

'Sit. Miss Sarah, sit.'

And so it was that I began to sit with these children. The more I sat, the more I discovered I was slowly beginning to reconnect to life again and all due to the unrelenting insistence of a dirty faced little Indian boy named Raaj.

As I allowed myself more and more of the physical interactions with these poor unfortunate children, emotionally, little by little my frozen heart began to thaw. I continued to spend my quiet time up on the hill, just outside the orphanage and to the astonishment of all, including Melissa, Lama Ngawan was now also in the habit of sitting with me.

I felt a growing comfort around him, so much so that the next time the silence was finally broken by his words, I was far better prepared to respond, or so I thought at the time. On that particular day when Lama chose to once again speak to me towards the end of a lengthy period of silence, the same question was asked.

'What do you see, Sarah?'

I had often reflected on what I *should* have said last time so much so that this time I was armed with a better response. I began describing exactly what I did see.

'I see poor discarded orphans. I see poverty and dust.'

Lama looked ahead and did not reply, so I went on.

'I see children easily born to parents that either had nothing, died or just didn't want them. I see sadness.'

Lama gently nodded his head and replied, 'I see none of that, Sarah.'

I looked back to the orphanage slightly puzzled by his response and again, right in front of me, I observe the poverty that is glaringly obvious. I feel sad as I observe the unloved, discarded children who have nothing; no home, no possessions, no family, no one to love them. The irony of what I am seeing is not lost on me and I feel suffocated by the heavy weight of the injustice of it all, for them, but mostly for me. I feel slightly annoyed at this monk who presumes to know me, and what I should and should not see. I look to him and ask in a slightly defensive voice, 'What should I see?'

'That is a question only you can answer, Sarah,' he replied, as he went back to his meditation.

I know the lesson for today is over. Later that day over dinner I talk to Melissa about my encounter.

'What does he want me to see, Melissa?'

'You will know when you see it,' she said in an infuriating way. 'He is teaching you what you need to know right now.'

I am tired and annoyed, and I really have no desire for mind games, so I make my excuses and leave the dining area early and head toward bed. I decide that I won't go to the hill tomorrow, but in the morning my desire to discover more about this intriguing man leads me back. This time he is already there. I sit beside him and don't wait for an invitation to speak.

'I see children playing in the dirt. I see poverty,' I say with defiance.

'You look, but you don't see, Sarah.' After a long pause he said, 'Look closer.'

And he walked away.

I put my head in my hands in annoyance and frustration and once again I had no idea what I was trying to achieve by being here.

The next day, again, I go to the hill and Lama arrives five minutes later. Today he greets me with a smile.

'Glad to see you have returned, Sarah,' he said as if he can read my mind and understand my frustration.

I ask if I may ask him a question.

He smiles and says, 'It appears you can, would you like to ask me another?'

I begin to tell him of my story. At first, all I wanted was his advice, his wisdom and understanding. I wanted to ask him "why me?" but instead, I began to speak the words that had remained buried that now flowed freely. It seemed as though I was unable to stop. I spoke of my heartfelt desire to have children of my own and the way this nightmare had touched everything in my life. I spoke of how it had destroyed my marriage, my work, my relationships and I spoke of 'my George'. After I had spilled out my lengthy monologue I again wanted to ask him "why me?" I wanted to ask him what could possibly be gained by taking the life of an innocent unborn child? I wanted to ask why God was so cruel? But, I didn't, I couldn't. Instead I just sat in silence and wept.

Lama sat in silence beside me staring ahead and did not speak.

After I composed myself I again found my voice and finally asked my question, 'Why me? What did I do to deserve this? Am I a bad person? Why me of all people, why me? What is my life all about— what else is there for me if I'm not to be a mother? It's all I've ever wanted, it's all I know how to be.'

My tears had stopped, the emotion of my words had finally been released and I felt numb again as I waited for a reply that was slow to come.

'Why not you, Sarah?'

I'm completely stunned by his reply.

Moments pass, and I cannot find my voice. I stand and begin to leave, half expecting him to say something else, anything else, but he doesn't.

For the next two days I avoid the hill. I ponder what was said and the harshness of those words. I begin to think about the meaning behind them, and as I do I move through a gamut of emotions from anger and sadness to guilt. Perhaps I *am* a bad person, the words of the nuns again ring in my ears. '*We are all sinners, Sarah*', but the question still remains. *Why me? Surely, I'm no more a sinner than the next person. I have tried to live a good and Christian life. Why me?* As I reflect on that question I realise I have actually said it out loud. I look around me to see who may have heard my words only to find my little shadow Raaj looking at me with a puzzled expression.

'You are indeed blessed, Miss Sarah. Why not you?'

The words from this ten-year-old boy lead me to feel ashamed.

'I'm sorry, Raaj. It would seem that I have lost myself lately.'

'That's okay, Miss Sarah," Raaj replied with a cheeky grin. 'I can help you find what you have lost. Samanera-Tseten says the Buddha teaches nothing is lost in the universe.'

'Then Samanera-Tseten is very wise.' I gently squeeze his shoulders as I turn to walk toward the dining area.

The next day I return to the hill, but Lama does not attend. I sit for a while and look and ask myself —*What do you see, Sarah?* I really look, but still come up with just the same. *Nothing!* Perhaps I'll do better tomorrow. I make my way back to the orphanage.

The children are excited to see me back so soon.

'Play with us, Miss Sarah.'

I notice children all over the world love a bat and a ball.

'Okay,' I relent. 'Just for ten minutes.'

Thirty minutes later, I finally take my leave with a smile on my face as it dawns on me that the children won that one.

Days turned into weeks and life in the orphanage was comfortably repetitious. I was developing a deep fondness for the children and I even began assisting with some of the afternoon classes, much to the joy of Raaj and certain other children who were never far from my side whenever I was in the yard. As the weeks passed, I was slowly beginning to see a different side to this place. I was spending more time with Stephanie and David and less time in the kitchen. As much as I first resisted forming attachments, I realised I was developing strong friendships with them both. I was also seeing a side to Melissa that was unexpected. It was obvious that she loved these children, all of them. She was tolerant and patient with them, and I was observing the caring, loving and very capable attitude of my mother alive and well within my previously wayward sister. During these weeks I came to almost depend on my frequent meetings with Lama Ngawan. There were days of course, during our meetings on the hill, when there was nothing but silence between us but even silence seemed somehow comforting when around this elderly monk.

On one occasion, as I approached the hill to find Lama there ahead of me, he nodded in greeting and before I had time to sit he said, 'Come, we will walk.'

I began to talk, and he said gently, 'Do not speak, Sarah. Observe.'

We walked on in silence, through the little village that lay beyond the walls of the orphanage and I noticed the beautiful colours that form part of the tapestry of this place. There were small market stalls along the road sides where the local farmers sold their produce, and women who wove and sold the most beautiful fabrics and of course, the ever-present smell of spices. The village was small but busy and the people were friendly. The local people showed great respect for this monk, bowing their heads with palms pressed together and fingers pointing upward in a prayer-like gesture, but some I noticed with astonishment also poked out their tongues. This gesture didn't seem to disturb Lama at all, in fact he respectfully nodded toward each of them as he continued on his journey. I wanted to ask him what it meant that many of these locals were poking out their tongues toward him, but I remained silent as I had been instructed.

Melissa later explained that when a person sticks out their tongue in greeting, it is to demonstrate to the observer that they are not the reincarnation of the cruel 9th century Tibetan King who happened to have a black tongue. Curious, I thought when Melissa explained this to me but 'when in Rome' I said as I cheekily stuck out my tongue at her like I had done so many times when I was a child for completely different reasons. Melissa, never to be outdone very quickly did the same and we both laughed and then she hugged me and told me, 'I've missed you, Sis'. When my walk with Lama came to an end that day he turned to me, placing his hands together and bowed his head and silently walked away.

'Wait,' I said. 'I need to speak to you,' but he did not turn around.

A few more weeks passed and one morning as I sat silently beside Lama, he asked the same question which was now predictable.

'What do you see, Sarah?'

It seemed he would continue asking until I gave him the answer he was looking for.

'I see what I saw last week, and the week before and the week before that. The orphanage, dusty children …'

With more authority than I had heard in his voice before, he said, 'Look closer, Sarah, open your mind. Do not see with your eyes, observe with your soul. Close your eyes, and *now* see.'

I obediently closed my eyes and sat in silence. A minute passed, and I realise that the poverty, dust and sadness of discarded children had all vanished. Instead I feel the warmth of the sun and a gentle breeze on my skin. I notice the warmth of the air in my nostrils as I breathe in and I smell the scent of spices on the breeze that are coming from the orphanage kitchen. I hear the sound of children playing and I am astonished to notice that I have heard these very sounds so many times before at my own school as I patrolled the playground on yard duty. When this thought dawns on me I notice a slight smile automatically beginning to appear on my face. I continue to sit with my eyes closed and feel for the first time in a very long time a real sense of calm and clarity flooding through my body. I don't want to open my eyes or speak because I want to hold on to this feeling; I don't want it to go. The tension I have held in my body for so long, without even realising it, begins to noticeably melt away as my brow softens and my shoulders begin to drop into a more relaxed position.

Minutes pass, with my eyes closed I say, 'I hear laughter. I hear the sounds of children playing, not poor children, not orphan children, just children. They sound happy and joyful. I smell the aroma of food being prepared for them.'

I sense Lama looking, but my eyes stay closed in an attempt to hold on to this feeling of calm that has descended upon me.

I hear his voice, 'How can this be, Sarah? These are orphans, they have no home, no parents, no family, they have been discarded. They have no possessions, they live in poverty. How can they be joyful and happy?'

I open my eyes. I finally get it. I simply nod and smile.

'Now, what do you see, Sarah?'

'I see happy children who are cared for, who have plentiful food and shelter. I see children who are grateful.'

I continue to watch as I notice Melissa in the yard below. She is playfully chasing the children in a fun attempt to gather them all in for their morning lesson. I notice for the first time the extent of the love that emanates from her towards these children and I feel humbled.

'I see a family.'

And, a wave of clarity flows over me.

'Well done, Sarah. Well done. True family is connected by love not by genetics.

When I look at these children, I see peace and joy. I see gratitude that is not based on possessions. This is a family of choice not requirement.'

I feel humbled by his words and wisdom.

'What have you learned?'

I have learned to look beyond what I see, and I have learned to be comfortable in silence.'

'Good, now you must learn more. You can never control what life gives you, what you *can* control is what you do with it. What you do and how you feel is always your choice. What will *you* choose, Sarah? Will you be a victim of this, or will you choose what these children have chosen?'

'I don't know what to do Lama, I feel like my life is in tatters. I don't know what there is for me now back home and it scares me. I'm not even sure where home is anymore. My entire life feels like it has been turned upside down.'

'I know about such change, Sarah. I too have endured much change, many years ago at a time of great turmoil. I survived, with the help of Maha-Thera Sanam, as will you. You have much to learn. Join us tomorrow in morning meditation. You are ready. Now, go and just be here and now, for there is no other place to be. You cannot be there when you are here, and you cannot be here when you are there. Learn to just be here now.'

Lama respectfully bowed his head and left me with my thoughts.

Five in the morning arrived all to quickly and to my complete disbelief I found myself bounding out of bed excitedly getting ready for meditation. *Who would have thought? Certainly not Matt.* I really hadn't been much of a morning girl, but nonetheless I arrived at the meditation hall ten minutes early. Children, volunteers and some of the monks had already begun to gather.

I took a purple cushion from the storage shelving and found myself a spot toward the back of the room to sit and get comfortable. I really wasn't sure of the process, but I was quickly instructed by one of the monks to just notice my breath. I start noticing, although, I am not quite sure what specifically I'm supposed to notice. As my instructor swishes past me again with orange robes making a now familiar sound, I ask through the silence a little too loudly 'what to do next'. His hand immediately goes to his mouth in a silent gesture designed to tell me to be the same. 'Just breathe and still your mind Ms Sarah. Don't talk!' he says with a frown.

I sit and breathe in the silence, my mind refuses to be still. Amidst the deafening silence my mind goes back to my lovely Californian bungalow in the beautiful seaside suburb of Aspendale, an entire world away from the Children of Hope Orphanage here in India. *Focus on your breath, Sarah,* I chastise myself. I open my eyes to have a little peek around to see if anyone else is finding this hard, only to discover my instructor looking directly at me. *Oh, crap.* I quickly shut them again. *Back to my breath. Yep, still breathing. Oh, thank God, at least that's working.* I try hard to hold back a wry smile that is forming on my face, lest the young monk is still looking at me with disapproval. *Breathe in. Breathe out. Breathe in. Breathe out.* It is becoming relaxing to breathe, perhaps I am doing something right, after all. I immediately remember countless evenings on the balcony back home after a big day of painting or renovating, when my whole body ached from the work of the day. When I finally allowed myself to stop and sit down it was as though my body instinctively knew to take a big breath in and smell the beautiful scent of sea air. It felt equally as instinctive for my whole body to then automatically exhale a big sigh of relief. I remember that feeling with fondness. It was comforting and there was a real feeling of achievement that was accompanied by a sense of a job well done.

Someone coughs in the room and it immediately brings me back to India but I quickly forget my breath again as I start to think about Matt. I wonder what he is doing? If he is coping. Mum had sent me an email that I had been able to access in the main town. It's been nine weeks since I left. Eleven weeks since my beautiful little baby boy left this world. Mum says Matt is coping. I know that probably means he is not.

Mum would never want to upset me by saying that Matt has fallen apart, yet I somehow know this is the truth. *He will move on,* I think to myself and it will be better in the long run, although as I think of Matt moving on I feel a great pang of sadness and regret. *Am I doing the right thing? I really didn't know anymore. I really miss his embrace that was always there to comfort me at times just like this. I'm becoming less and less sure about the choice I have made to walk away from him, but I try to convince myself that he will be better off. He can start anew and perhaps it is not too late for him to be the father he so deserves to be. I have no funds, no way of supporting myself, so I asked before I left that our home we have worked so hard on together be put up for sale. I can't bear the thought of strangers happily living in my house. It's just one more loss.*

This time I gratefully return to focusing on my breath to avoid the sadness consuming me that I fear may lead me to tears. *Not here. Breathe, Sarah ... breathe ... breathe. I wish Jane was here, she'd know what to say to make me feel better. Bugger, I've done it again* as I realise and try to focus on my breath.

This is harder than it looks. Breathe in. Breathe out. I should really reply to Mum's email, it's been a while and she will be worrying. Breathe in. Breathe out. How long do we need to sit here? Breathe in. Breathe out. It feels like I've been sitting for hours and my bum is beginning to hurt. Are we allowed to move ... ARHHHHH STOP thinking! How hard can this be? Breathe in. I just need to move a little ... everything is so quiet here ... my cushion makes a noise on the floor as I reposition myself ... *did anyone in the room not hear that? Oh, are we done yet? I'm no good at this. Breathe out. You can do it Sarah. Breathe in. Oh, for God's sake stop thinking—just breathe out. I wonder if anyone will notice if I quietly slip out? Breathe in—Right, I'm out of here, this isn't working.*

I make my way to the back of the room to make a discrete exit as quietly as I can. I leave my cushion on the floor, a dead giveaway. There's no way my exit will go unnoticed by the instructor even if everyone else in the room has become so absorbed in their meditation that they have suddenly all become deaf. I feel like a naughty school girl about to wag class. As I walk around the corner, slightly relieved and happily feeling like I have been pretty well undetected, I come face to face with Lama Ngawan.

Crap!

CHAPTER 15
GOING WITHIN
THE JOURNEY FROM THERE TO HERE

Lama Ngawan surveys my stunned face and calmly says, 'Challenging, is it not?'

I smile sheepishly as though I had just been caught out by the principal and reply, 'Yes.'

'That is so, but the question remains, are you ready for the challenge, Sarah, or will you continue to let your monkey mind rule?'

I say nothing and just look at him. *Monkey Mind? That's a little harsh.* I know he can see right through me.

'A little harsh you think?'

God, he can read my mind. He begins to walk as he continues talking, an unspoken invitation for me to accompany him, and so I do.

'The Buddha once said that the human mind is filled with drunken monkeys flinging themselves from tree to tree in every direction while constantly chattering. Does this sound familiar, Sarah? Taming the monkey mind will bring clarity and contentment. Make friends with your monkey mind, let it be heard. When it has been heard, let it be still. Do not fight it for the answers you seek are not out there.' He gestures to the court yard. 'They are not in there,' he then gestures to the meditation room. 'They are in here.'

He stops walking, turns to face me and places his palm directed toward the area of my heart. I detect a slightly warm sensation from it even though he has not touched me it's as though his hand is somehow radiating heat, it's tangible, surprising and comforting all at the same time.

Sarah, you have everything you need to find the answers you seek, but only in silence will you hear. When will you choose to listen?'

'Tomorrow?' I hesitantly reply.

'Tomorrow.' He turns and walks away.

This time I don't follow. *Okay tomorrow it is.*

The next day I return to the meditation hall. There is a different monk presiding. He's much younger and far less intimidating. I look about for Lama Ngawan, but he is nowhere to be seen. I arrive five minutes early and the younger monk comes to speak to me. I wonder if Lama Ngawan has asked him to watch over me, so I don't make an early getaway again, but whatever the reason, I am comforted by his friendly reassuring countenance.

'Hello, Miss Sarah,' he says with a large friendly smile. 'I am Banyu, my name means water. I have never been to the ocean though,' he says with an amused expression. 'I understand you desire to learn meditation.'

I'm not too sure that I desire to learn, but apparently, I am going to learn. Not to be rude I say politely, 'Yes, I didn't do so well yesterday.'

'Nor I,' he replies grinning a not befitting grin for a monk. 'I shall help you. When the monkey mind wanders, simply bring it back to the breath. Do not be bothered. Your mind is in the habit of wandering, you need to train it, just like you train a cheeky monkey that jumps all around.' He wildly gestures with his arms to demonstrate his point. 'The more you bring it back the less it is naughty.'

Another big grin, I think I'm going to like Banyu.

'The Buddha taught many different types of meditation, let us begin with one. Now please be comfortable, and we will begin.'

Banyu squats down beside me.

'Bring your attention into the present and you may like to stare at the Buddha statue right there.' He gestures to the front of the room. 'Really notice it now, Miss Sarah, the details, colours, notice your thoughts arising. let them come—let them go—without judgement.'

I look at the statue for a few minutes, and it is true that I do see things that previously went unobserved.

'Now close your eyes.' He pauses for maybe a minute. 'Now be fully aware of your body in this space, in this room. Release tensions from the body.'

He leads and directs my attention throughout my entire body and instructs me to be relaxed yet alert all at the same time.

'Excellent, Miss Sarah, now think, what is it you want to achieve from your meditation today, do you want to tame the monkey mind? Bring your awareness to your breath. Meditation is an alert state of focused attention, the opposite to sluggishness. Let your attention explore the breath as though you have never really noticed it before. Notice as you breath in—notice as you breathe out.'

Silent pause.

'Notice the space between the breath.'

Silence.

'Notice where the air travels.'

Silence.

'Notice the temperature of the air.'

Silence.

'Notice how the breath out relaxes you more deeply.'

Silence.

'Notice the movement in your body as you breathe.'

Silence.

'Now we will count the breath. Breathe in … one. Breathe out. Breathe in … two. Breathe out. Breathe in … three. Breathe out. Breathe in … four. Breathe out.'

Banyu continued to direct me until we reached ten breaths and then he instructed me to go back to one and begin again solo.

'Thoughts will come, Miss Sarah. You must take charge. When you are aware of thoughts you can return your attention to the breath.'

As I sat, to my astonishment I was enjoying the feeling of peace and tranquillity flowing through me. *Wow, Banyu, you're a star. Oops, monkey mind. Back to the breath.* I smiled.

For the next weeks Banyu instructed me on all things meditation and I was a good student. Meditation became my practice morning and night. As the weeks passed into months I found that I was actually looking forward to my meditations. There was something quite different about the feeling I experienced when I was meditating that was hard to define.

I slowly began to tame my monkey mind and as I did, I noticed more and more a kind of respite or time out from the constant repetitive and destructive thoughts that had plagued me for years. The sense of calm I found during my meditation seemed in some way to flow on through my non-meditation hours.

As I developed a sense of calm, I was also learning how to sort and process thoughts that were not helpful. I was even worrying less about what the future had in store for me as the previously everpresent feeling of anxiety seemed to almost miraculously dissipate in direct correlation to the amount of time I spent in meditation. My heavy sense of grief, however, was not so obliging, but even this seemed to dissipate during my sessions as I directed my attention away from these thoughts in those moments.

I discovered many interesting and unexpected things over the next two months of meditating twice, and sometimes more, every day. It seemed that my whole body was enjoying the process of meditation as my persistent aches and pains that I had endured for many years seemed to almost disappear. I had to admit life felt better in many ways. Perhaps, these monks were on to something. I discussed with Banyu the surprising added benefits I was noticing from my meditation practice and he again gave me his now familiar cheeky grin accompanied by a slight nod of his head. His look resembled the smile of a proud parent when their child takes their first step.

'Yes, Miss Sarah, it is true, the body desires to be at peace. You are now becoming aware of how your unhappy thoughts create an unhappy body, not surprising then, that the body functions best when the mind is at peace. Your meditation will benefit your body in many ways. When the mind is still, the heart is happy. When the heart is happy it grows in loving kindness. When the mind is still what else has the body to do but function and heal.'

Again, he gives me a knowing smile as though he has waited for me to finally understand.

'Meditation can relieve your pain better than any medications. The mind and the body are not separate, Miss Sarah, when the mind is not at peace the body is not at peace, but when the mind is calm the body returns to the business of functioning perfectly and this you are beginning to observe. A lesson well learned, Miss Sarah.'

Well whatever the reason, all I knew was that I was physically feeling better than I had in years, so I kept an open mind and continued to learn what I could. During these weeks of meditating and perfectly timed impromptu lessons from Banyu, I continued to venture up to the hill when I could. Lama Ngawan would be there on some days but not as often as before. He seemed happy to leave me in the care of Banyu during this time and so I happily settled into my new kind of normal.

I enjoyed the occasions Lama did make it to the hill. I was now beginning to understand just what a privilege it was to spend this private time with him and so I really began to be very present whilst in his company. Something that Banyu had taught me. My focus of attention was seemingly much improved with my ongoing medita-tion, my monkey mind, was on the way to being tamed. I wasn't there yet but I was finding my ability to really be *in* the conversa-tion rather than be elsewhere, was a great asset to my communi-cations.

It was on one such occasion while I was deep in contemplation that Lama spoke to me the words I had been dreading to hear.

'Sarah, your time here is nearing its end.'

I felt an instant surge of denial masquerading as anxiety in the pit of my stomach that felt somewhat like a physical blow that took my breath away. I instinctively opened my mouth to disagree, but quickly closed it again. Part of me knew that this was true, but there was another part of me that did not want to leave. The part that was afraid to leave; afraid of the unknown. The part that still had no idea of exactly what there was for me back home. The very same part that didn't even know where home was anymore. Last month I received an email that my beloved home had been sold and a few weeks later, after a very short settlement, a sum of money was deposited in my account. I wasn't even sure of the details. I didn't want to know or think about what the implications of that were. I have been here for nearly five months now. Matt had attempted to contact me many times, he even wanted to come over here to talk but I ignored his requests and after no response from me he eventually stopped trying.

After a significant pause in our conversation, which allowed me time to process all my thoughts, I looked to Lama who was studying me intently.

'What about Melissa?' I said, knowing this was a futile attempt to appease my anxieties and make my point. 'She's been here for years.'

'This is her path, Sarah, she has chosen this life, you have run away from yours.'

This felt harsh, but deep within I knew he was right. I have come to learn that Lama does not sugarcoat things. I sit in silence.

'What is *my* path? I ask as though I expect him to give me the answer, but I know he won't.

'You will know, Sarah. Meditate on it. Your journey is of value. Your experiences have taught you much. How will you give value to those experiences? You are a teacher Sarah, now go and teach.'

Lama rises and leaves me to consider his words, and as usual his words are powerful. Something in me is ignited at hearing those words. I replay them in my mind: *How will I give value to my experience? How will I give value to my experience?* Almost like a lightning bolt from heaven I suddenly feel as though I have a purpose. Giving value to my experience, means giving value to my beautiful little baby George's existence. Making his life stand for something. Telling the world, he was here, he existed, and he added value to the world simply by his presence. This was to be my purpose. I suddenly felt inspired, George's presence would not go unnoticed. He was important, and he would give value to the world.

For the next week I pondered Lama's words. *How exactly was I to give value to my experiences?* I thought about it day and night. I tried to still my monkey mind during my meditations, but thoughts managed to creep in and I allowed them, after all Lama had told me to meditate on it. Who knows in the stillness I may find the answer I was looking for, and as it turned out that is exactly what happened.

One week to the day, after hearing Lama's words I had an epiphany that was to forever change my life. I would give value to my experiences and give value to George by helping other women have children. I would use my valuable experience to teach others the things I have learned. I would spread my message far and wide. Do not wait for life to be perfect because time is precious and not to be taken for granted, but there was another important message that was dawning on me and this was personal. It suddenly became apparent to me that *I* was of value; *me* and my life in and of itself. Not the me I had always imagined me to be, the teacher who would one day be a mother and run a household full of children just like my own beautiful mum had. Not the image of myself that I had believed for so long that somehow gave me an identity and a purpose, but the *me* who was just Sarah: an individual, a single standalone person. I was valuable! My life had purpose and I could make a difference. I could exist and be of value with or without children. I was whole, I was valuable and now I had a purpose that was perhaps always meant to be. I was to make a difference in this world because I had something important to contribute. As this realisation began to filter through every fibre of my being like a wave of conscious aware-ness, I realised that I could offer hope to women by helping them find their purpose. I could offer hope by letting women know they have value with or without children just as I did. I would lead by example, but again the question remained, how?

Lama's words began to ring loudly *Fight the battles you can win Sarah, for to do anything else is futile.*

It wasn't long before the answer came to me. The more I thought about my goals of what I hoped to achieve, the more the solution began to come into focus. I would not let my past pain and disap-pointment define my future. I would use my experience to add value to the world. If the Sarah I was reinventing was to help others I would need a place from which to do it. I began to imagine what this place would be like and as I focused more and more on this, an image began to develop in my mind. It was an image of a tranquil space away from the distractions of everyday life. A retreat of sorts specifically designed to educate infertile women and to support those who had finished their journey to discover that there is life after infertility and IVF and *that* life has real value. *That's it* I thought. *I will create a retreat!*

My mind automatically went to the money that had been placed into my bank account from the sale of our home, and for the first time I could think of this without the heavy melancholy I had previously experienced. Even the loss of my home now seemed to have a purpose. I haven't even bothered to look at the amount of money that is in my bank account but now I was interested. I'm sure it wasn't much, but it would be a start.

I excitedly began to think about all the details that would eventually create my retreat. Where it would be, what it would look like, what spaces would be needed, the atmosphere I wanted to create. It would be a place of safety, understanding and acceptance. I thought about who else would be involved, and on and on and on. In my mind I explored so many possibilities, even the name of my retreat would in some way commemorate the life of my precious George. He would never be forgotten. My mind was abuzz with ideas and I knew right then that this would become a reality.

The "Sarah of old" would have scoffed at such a thought and would have immediately dismissed such a grandiose idea. She would have questioned herself as to just who she was to dare to do such a thing, but not anymore. Life was precious and not to be wasted or taken for granted. Lama Ngawan whilst in exile as a displaced person created this orphanage out of nothing. He did it for the children because there was a true need for it. I will create my retreat for all the women just like me and the men just like Matt because there is also a true need for it. It will help to build families and just as importantly, it will help to save families. I want to help couples survive the emotional rollercoaster that is infertility and help them to keep sight of the bigger picture. I want to give them the tools that I have learnt that will enable them to stay focused on what they already have that is of value rather than what they don't have. I will teach them to close their eyes and see through a different lens.

As these thoughts flooded through my mind I felt a strong sense of purpose emerging that was to be the foundation stones of my new venture. I was also slowly beginning to understand all that I had lost, not through age and wasted time and not through genetic necessity, but through choice. I thought of Matt and instinctively began to realise that which I previously could not see through the fog of my grief. We were already a family, we were already whole. The love that I had for this man, the love that I have always had, the love that I had denied for so long now immediately and uncontrollably surged through me like an unstoppable tsunami.

Oh, my God, what have I done?

Was it too late?

CHAPTER 16
ACCEPTANCE AND FAREWELL

My last week at the orphanage was tinged with excitement and sadness both at the same time.

It was time to go home. I knew it, I could feel it. The thought no longer terrified me. There was an inevitability in it that was somewhat comforting because I now had a sense of purpose that excited me to the core of my being. There was a motivation and passion that I was discovering driving me now, and it seemed as though there was a constant stream of endless possibilities that were presenting themselves to me the more I thought about what my retreat would be. I would need to start looking for a property when I got home, but first I needed to enjoy my last days here.

I had learned a lot during my now nearly five and a half months here in India, and I would surely miss my new-found friends and this place that I had come to love and that now seemed like home.

Raaj, my dirty-faced little side kick was particularly upset that I was to leave him. During my time here, other than when I ventured out of the orphanage to the hill, he was never far from my side. He even worked with me in the kitchen or the laundry if he was not in classes. I tried to reassure him that we would meet again, and it was not goodbye for ever, but he was not so convinced. He had seen a great deal in his short life and I think he had learned that others could not always be relied upon to do as they said they would do. To be honest he may actually be right, I may never come back to India. I may never see him again, but I could not break his little heart by telling him that. I had grown so fond of Raaj that the thought of leaving him behind was truly hard.

Lama Ngawan had been pleased that I had found a valuable way to validate my experience and I would honour him, George, and myself, by making my vision a reality. I feel so blessed to have had his tutelage, and I will truly miss him.

The day before I was to leave Lama came to me and bowed his head as he placed his hands together in a sign of prayer.

'Namaste, Sarah you have learned well. You will be missed.'

'I will miss being here.'

'I wish to give you something.' He reaches into his robes and pulls out something that looks like a small gift, wrapped in orange cloth and tied with string. 'Open it, Sarah.'

Within the parcel is a small cord-like bracelet with a knot tied into it. I look at Lama and he smiles.

'This is a traditional practice of Lamas of the Buddhist religion. I have tied the knot in the cord and I have blown a mantra into the knot making a blessing for you, Sarah. My blessing is for you to create your vision of value, and while you hold on to this bracelet you will always have me with you.'

I feel humbled by the gesture and place my hands together, bow my head with tears forming in my eyes and say, 'Namaste, dear Lama Ngawan. I shall treasure it always.'

'Namaste, Sarah, let us walk.'

We walked. One last journey to the hill, one last memory to treasure. One last goodbye. I was not to see Lama after that time. He had duties to attend to in the morning when I was to leave, but I think he wanted it this way. He had said his goodbyes in the way he preferred; respectfully, privately.

That night in the dining area the children had practised a special farewell song and they sang it beautifully whilst dancing and clapping. My heart was so full of joy as I watched them that I had a physical sensation in my body that wanted to burst out of my chest. As I acknowledged the extent of my joy and love for these children I was struck by the startling realisation of just how far I had come since I arrived within these walls.

The children presented me with drawings and letters, and after a special celebratory meal of steamed bread, noodle soup and vegetable curry and as a special treat, a serve of Cheser Mog, a Tibetan rice dish made of yak butter, brown sugar, raisins and salt, I made my way to my room for the last time. I felt a mixture of excitement and sadness at the prospect of leaving this place that had been my home for so long. I didn't know what tomorrow would bring, but I did know I would face all the challenges one by one as they presented themselves. I had no doubt there would be challenges but I would not waste this precious moment worrying about them. I snuggled down into bed completely contented and fell to sleep.

The next morning after breakfast it was time to go. Melissa helped take my case to the bus as I said my goodbyes to everyone. David and Stephanie, now cherished friends were waiting at the bus when I arrived.

'Travel safe,' David said, as he put out his hand to shake mine.

I stepped toward him and gave him a full-on hug and when he sheepishly stepped away looking slightly embarrassed he smiled and cleared his throat and said, 'Right then,' as he rubbed his hands together, not quite sure what else to do next. His English upbringing it seems has left him a little unsure of acceptable protocol for embracing a woman under such circumstances. Stephanie and I exchanged a knowing glance and smiled.

'David you're blushing,' pointed out Stephanie, now laughing as she playfully taunted him before turning to embrace me herself.

We hugged for the longest moment, neither of us wanting to let go first.

She quietly whispered in my ear in an emotional voice, 'You better stay in touch,' and then as if to reduce the seriousness of the moment she cheekily said, 'I want a job at your retreat.' She kissed me on the cheek and stepped away.

Melissa was standing in the background during all of my goodbyes and gently reminded me that we would need to get on our way soon.

'You've got ten minutes, Sarah,' she said.

I was once again about to make the long journey back to the airport in the old mini-bus that had so long ago begun my pilgrimage here in India. I was now so well acquainted with it, it seemed perfect that I should make this, my last journey, in this old squeaky but ever so reliable vehicle that had been meticulously washed by the children in preparation for my departure.

I look into the small crowd of children and others that had gathered for Banyu and I spot him approaching me. I had hoped I would see his happy face one last time.

He walked up to me and said with a warm smile, 'Travel well, Miss Sarah.'

Buddhists believe it is better to travel well than to arrive.

'I will, Banyu,' I replied with a respectful bow of my head and hands placed as though in prayer. This was now such a familiar and heartfelt gesture for me, I found myself doing it almost instinctively.

'The Buddha teaches the whole secret to existence is to have no fear,' he said. 'Now, it is time, go, Miss Sarah, as you are ready. Rise up, be grateful and be of value to the world as is your destiny.' He then bowed his head and said, 'Namaste,' as he turned and left me to say my farewells to the children.

Knowing time is short I look around me for Raaj and notice him standing back a little, patiently waiting his turn to speak to me.

I walk to him and he smiles, 'May love and truth eternal guide you.'

'Raaj, that is so beautiful. Thank you!'

'The words are from a farewell song we learnt in school, Miss Sarah. I will treasure the golden hours we have spent together,' he says proudly, 'that is also from the song.'

I do my best not to giggle as it would crush him.

'I will treasure the golden hours we have spent together also, Raaj.'

I notice that he has made an extra effort to wash his face and knees which are now free of the familiar dirt smears that generally accompany his early morning cricket game.

'I will miss you, Miss Sarah, I will miss you greatly. I have a gift for you.'

'Raaj, you shouldn't have got me a gift,' I protest, but he reaches into his pocket and pulls out a smooth irregular shaped gemstone.

'I found it in the gravel when they dug out the old well. I told Lama Ngawan and he told me that it was a moonstone and it was meant for me as I had found it. Now, Miss Sarah, it is meant for you. I have polished it with sand and oil so that it shines like the moon to light your path home.'

I take the stone and admire the beauty of it.

'It does indeed shine, Raaj. You have done a beautiful job of polishing it. I will treasure it always.'

I give him a hug and notice when I pull away that he has tears forming in his eyes, which he quickly brushes away as he stands tall as if to tell me he is a man and will be all right.

'I will miss you greatly too, Raaj.'

The rest of the children push in to have one last hug and goodbye, as Melissa grabs me by the arm and begins to shepherd me toward the passenger seat saying, 'if we don't go now, Sarah, we will have to go through all this again tomorrow'. I jump in the mini-bus and it splutters into life on the third attempt and we slowly begin to drive away with a parade of children running behind shouting and waving goodbye. As we drive around the corner I get one last glimpse of the yard and notice Raaj standing back, not part of the happy excited group of children, just standing all alone, silently staring as we turn out of sight.

'Will you look after Raaj for me, Melissa? Keep a special eye on him. I'm worried about him.'

'Of course, Sarah, I'll look out for him, he'll be fine,' she touched my hand to reassure me.

The journey to the airport seemed to fly by so much faster than I had remembered it to be the first time I travelled these roads. The daylight seemed to make the journey more interesting as I could clearly see the colours and the hustle and bustle of this busy country. I now no longer felt like a stranger in a strange place. I now felt like I belonged here. I was now a part of the rich, transformative, colourful tapestry of India and it would always hold a cherished place in my heart. Who would have thought so much could change in such a short time? The Sarah who arrived emotionally kicking and screaming, literally because there was absolutely nowhere else to go, now can hardly believe her good fortune for having had this experience. It was meant to be. A power greater than me; The Universe, God, Buddha, I really don't know which, and part of me wonders if it is not the same thing anyway, has guided me here so that I can make a difference in the world. I will meet that challenge and I will help others on their journeys, but I will also give value to my experience, so that it will honour the life of a baby boy named George.

The closer we got to Delhi airport the busier it seemed to get. We eventually arrived, checked in and made our way to the departure area. This time I was not so stunned by the sights and sounds of this busy airport. This time I was comfortably familiar with the people, the smells and the customs. I had now come to understand just what kept my sister here, in fact I had come to understand my sister. The Melissa I now know and understand is so far removed from the Melissa I thought I knew. No longer was she the self-involved, uncaring Melissa of our childhood, now the woman who stood before me was someone I was so proud to call my sister. She was someone who was caring and loving, someone who gave of her time and her heart, someone who would show up unexpectedly at your door to rescue you even when you didn't realise you needed rescuing. She was someone who could be depended upon to be there when you needed her the most and she was someone who strangely reminded me so much of our mother.

It was now time to go through customs, and this part of my journey I would do solo. I was feeling quite emotional, I was excited and sad all at the same time. I was sad to leave India and sad to leave my sister who I was just getting to really know again, but I was also flying back to start a new life and see if there was anything left of my old life to salvage, and this thought was very daunting. Everything had changed since I left, but I couldn't allow myself to think about that now. I hugged Melissa and didn't want to let go. Tears began to well and Melissa smiled as she pulled away and began to poke fun at me as if to lighten the mood.

'Oh, you big Sissy-La-La,' she laughed and then poked her tongue out at me in traditional Tibetan greeting to assure me she did not have a black tongue and was not evil.

It certainly did the trick. I laughed at the funny face she was pulling as I told her that she was only supposed to do that when you meet someone, not when you say goodbye.

'Oh, smarty pants, Banyu has taught you well, little Sis. Go on now, on your way. Travel well, Sarah. I love you and I'll see you soon.'

She smiled a big genuine smile and gave me one more hug and said, 'Go and take on the world, Sarah. I know you'll be great. Give my love to Mum and Dad and tell them I'll come visit soon.'

Then she turned and walked away, turning for one last quick wave. I'm sure I could see her crying.

I made my way through customs and then had the long wait until boarding. We had allowed plenty of time. Often customs are an arduous process of long queues and delays, but fortunately all went as smoothly as possible at Delhi Airport.

Soon it was time to board my 1 pm Air India flight home via Sydney. I boarded and found my seat which was a window seat on the left side of the plane. I got out my book and put it in the seat pocket. I didn't feel much like reading, so I settled myself and closed my eyes and took a few meditative breaths to clear my racing mind. It still amazed me to discover just how effective even a couple of breaths were at settling my mind and allowing me peace and clarity. *Why wasn't this being taught in schools?* I wondered. As I opened my eyes, I found that my neighbour, a middle aged Australian man, was staring at me.

'Nervous luv?' he asked. 'Don't worry we are safe as houses. My son is a pilot you know, safer than driving a car he says. You'll be fine.'

It's funny how people make assumptions, I quietly smile at him, nod and then turn to look out the window. We have a thirteen-hour journey ahead of us and I'm in no mood to talk the whole way. Our plane begins to taxi to the runway. Ground staff are everywhere loading and unloading other planes. I capture my last glimpses of

India before we are airborne and all too soon India becomes a colourful and aromatic memory.

As I settle in for the long haul back to Sydney Australia, I think *well, what now Sarah Murphy?* But the exhaustion of the last few days arising from planning my departure and the excitement of all things to come combined with the sad farewells suddenly begins to show and as I surrender to it, my eyes close and my last thoughts before I drift off to sleep are of Matt.

My flight arrived into Sydney around 8:30 p.m. and I quickly made my way through customs to my connecting flight to Melbourne. Jane will be waiting at the gate lounge for me. It's probably been the longest period of time that we haven't seen each other. So much has changed for me over the past months and I could hardly wait to see her to tell her everything. Jane wanted me to stay at her place until I got settled and I agreed. At this stage I really didn't know where else to go. Mum and Dad were getting older now and even though I know they would have welcomed me back home with open arms, something in me just felt wrong about that. I was not just going to go back home and assume my old life. I wasn't the same person who hopped on that plane and ran away from life. I was Sarah Murphy; Mother of George Murphy, and I was coming home to make a difference.

It was eleven when I rounded the corner of the disembarkation bridge to see my best friend's smiling face in front of the waiting small crowd. I could hardly contain my excitement as I saw her. Emotion spread through my body like an electric current and I felt the tears of joy rapidly welling in my eyes.

'You look amazing,' she said as she embraced me. 'How was your flight? Are you hungry? Have you had anything to eat? Tell me everything, how are you, Sarah?'

I had no time to answer one question before the next was fired off and I was delighted to see that nothing had changed with Jane. My beautiful and reliable friend was here for me as usual and at that moment I knew everything would be all right.

Tullamarine Airport was fairly busy for a Saturday night, but we managed to get my bags, jump in the car and leave it all behind us fairly quickly. "Welcome to Melbourne" I see the sign on the side of the Tullamarine freeway zip past me as we make our way to Jane's place; a very comfortable two-bedroom town house in South Melbourne, perfectly positioned due to its proximity to the hospital. Jane was often called out at all hours, so she needed to live close to the city, but true to form she still managed to stay by the water of Port Phillip Bay. We both loved the water. I had so many fond memories of growing up with Jane at the beach. There was some-thing about the water, and the salt air that just seemed to bring clarity.

Jane and I chatted as we continued on down Nepean Highway and before I realised it we were in Brighton.

'Where are you going, Jane? You've missed the turn off.'

She just smiled and said, 'We are going to Rye. I hope you don't mind. I have a new beach house and I think it is the perfect place for us to catch up on the last few months, and *I* have a week off work!'

'Wow, Jane. Yes, that sounds wonderful.'

It's perfect. How does this woman know me so well? Mum and Dad were not aware that I had come home, in fact none of my family were. I really hoped that they would understand my decision, but it really didn't matter to me. The Sarah of old would never have done such a thing, but I was not the Sarah of old and I needed time to think. I had asked Melissa to keep it quiet for the time being and naturally she agreed. She had a certain way of understanding what I needed right now, and I didn't have to explain it to her. I wanted to do things my way; to get clear about what I was to do and how I was to do it. I needed this clarification before I was to subject myself to the influences of other people's opinions. I would not listen to any negativity about what I was to do. I could not entertain it. I had learned in India that my thoughts were very powerful on my outcomes and I was not going to let other people's doubts affect my outcomes. The choice was mine. I looked at the knotted cord bracelet around my wrist and thought of Lama's words: *Close your eyes, Sarah, and see with your heart. How will you give value to your experience?* His words floated through my consciousness as the lights of Cheltenham sped past me.

It was late by the time we finally arrived into Rye. All was quiet as we turned into a tea tree lined drive. I couldn't see much due to the darkness, but the house seemed to be nestled in amongst coastal vegetation and from the outside at least it looked fairly modest.

'Let's hit the hay. You must be exhausted.' Jane said, 'I'll show you around tomorrow.'

She led me to my room just down the entry hall and a short way around the corner to the right. She turned on the light and gave me a brief tour of my room; spare pillows and blankets and somehow, I had lucked the ensuite.

'Jane, I hope this is not your room,' I began to protest.

'No, I'm upstairs, this is all yours. I'll show you the rest of the house tomorrow. Sleep in as long as you need, I may pop into town for a couple of things so don't worry if you can't find me. Good night, Sarah. Sleep tight, don't let the bed bugs bite.' She laughed and walked out.

I doubt there would be bed bugs here I thought, as I looked around me, I could have been forgiven for thinking I was in a posh hotel. I yawned and began to realise how tired I was. A quick brush of my teeth and I fell into bed, happy to be back on home soil.

Goodnight Jane.

CHAPTER 17
HOME

I slept like a log that night. It was ten in the morning before I opened my eyes and looked at the bedside clock. At first, I had no idea where I was. I looked around this comfortably appointed room as it dawned on me, I was back in Australia. I took a few moments to orientate myself and decided I should get up. I opened the block out blinds and light flooded into the room. As I looked out the window I caught glimpses of the ocean through the trees. I'm sure Jane said we were not too far from St Andrews Beach. I noticed my room had a small deck connected to it via a sliding full-length window and I took the opportunity to slip out and breathe in the sea air. I needed to meditate, it was a must these days and I couldn't imagine starting my day without it, even at ten. I smiled to myself as I wondered, *what would Banyu think?* I sat for a quiet moment. *No time like the present.* Just a quick one this morning, after all, what's another twenty minutes. I settled myself out on the deck and breathed in the salt sea air and quickly went into a deep state of meditation.

When I completed my meditation, I felt far more alert and ready to face the day. I crept out of my room still in my pyjamas to investigate the rest of the house and to find Jane. I noticed three other doors that were possibly bedrooms. I knew Jane's room was upstairs and as we were the only ones in the house I felt free to check them out. Two were double bedrooms, both slightly smaller than mine without the balcony and ensuite but equally comfortable it seemed, and the third door led to a bathroom, well-appointed with a massive spa bath. Excellent I thought, I will be using that I'm sure. I noticed at the end of the hall another door that had been hidden from view right opposite the stair return. I opened the door to find a narrow laundry with an external door leading to a small utility area. The hills hoist standing proudly in the middle and to the left an outside shower to wash off the sand after the beach I supposed. I was impressed with the little beach shack, Jane had done well. I left the laundry and followed the stairs up to discover a huge open kitchen living area with a massive outside deck perfectly positioned to take in the sea views, it was stunning. Jane's beach house was not the modest little shack that it had appeared to be, nestled in the dark behind native tea tree scrub. I step out onto the deck to survey the view.

Jane appeared from an adjoining room and brightly said, 'Good Morning sleepy head, how did you sleep?'

'Like a log. This place is amazing, Jane.'

'It's all about the ocean for me. I can come here and really unwind. I love it. Bought it not long after you left, had to do something with my spare time when I didn't have Aspendale to go to anymore.'

Suddenly I feel a pang of sadness and it apparently showed in my eyes, because Jane immediately said, 'Oh, God, I'm such an idiot, sorry Sarah.' She hugged me and continued, 'Let's eat. I've been into Rye and I've got some of your favourite cereal, fruit, fresh coffee and juice, what would you like? Oh, and I also got some Rye bread. See what I did there? Rye bread?'

'Funny. Good to see you haven't changed much.'

I enjoy the comfort of my dear friend. It's great to see she hadn't changed a bit, and that was the wonderful thing about Jane and I; we would not see each other for months and then we just picked up exactly where we left off. There's something so reassuring about a friendship like that, it's dependable. We sat out on the deck for hours on the solid hardwood dining table and chair setting. The sun was shining and there was a gentle sea breeze. We ate, and we talked, and we talked, and we ate some more. There was a lot to catch up on and Jane was eager to hear all.

We talked about my time in India, the people I met, the experiences I had. I told her about Lama Ngawan, Banyu and all that I had learned from these amazing people. I talked about my very proper English friend David and how sweet he was. We talked about Stephanie and all the other volunteers, and I spoke about Raaj, my little shadow and how I was worried about him now I was gone. I showed Jane my precious moonstone and told her how he had found it in the gravel and hand polished it for me with sand and oil. It must have taken him so long to do it. His cheeky smile came to mind and I thought of him trying to be so grown up when I left, but knowing his little heart was breaking was still making me feel so sad.

There was so much to say, and Jane quietly listened as Jane did. She was as good at listening as she was at talking, but she seemed to have a gift for knowing which to do when. She asked about Melissa and how it had gone knowing all too well our previously distant and somewhat tumultuous relationship. I began to describe how Melissa was so different to the Melissa we both knew and had grown up with. The selfish Melissa who was all about herself and to be honest the Melissa that neither of us was particularly fond of. It was almost as if she were a different person, or perhaps I had never really taken the time to get to know her. I said how she was well suited for the work she was doing at the orphanage, and that it was valuable work and how she was making a difference in the lives of so many. I looked at Jane's surprised and somewhat sceptical face as I told her I was so proud of Melissa.

Jane just looked at me incredulously as though I'd gone completely mad and said, 'Who are you and what have you done with Sarah? No seriously. What have they done to you over there? Quick, you must need coffee,' she then poured me a strongly brewed cup of steaming aromatic rich brew.

'It's true Jane, people can change, it's hard to believe I know but Melissa has probably brought me back to life and I will be forever grateful that she reached out to me when I was drowning in self-pity and remorse and pulled me to the safety of the most unlikely place I could have ever imagined. My life has changed, my perspective has changed and now I truly know what this has all been about. I know what I am supposed to do from here Jane. I understand finally how I can take something positive from this experience. It's the only way I can make sense of it, the only way I can move forward from it and it's the only way I can give value to it and let go of the pain. I'm grateful for the lessons I have learned and I'm going to give value to George's existence, and I would really love your support, because I'm not sure how I'm going to do it on my own.'

Jane reached out and took my hand, 'Of course, I'll be here for you, Sarah. I'm pretty blown away by the transformation in you that's all. I think we can both safely say that you were pretty messed up when you left, and I don't mind saying that I was really worried about you, we were all worried about you, but you somehow seem to have turned it all around. We're mates Sarah, best mates, we've fought all our battles side-by-side and I'll be right beside you through this too. Actually, even when I'm not right beside you I want to support you in any way I can until you get back on your feet, so I want you to know that you're welcome to stay here if you want, for as long as you need.'

'What! No, Jane I couldn't impose on you like that.'

'Oh, rubbish we both know you can, cut the crap Sarah, I want you to if you want to.'

'Oh, my God, that is amazing.'

My head begins to spin with possibilities. I can begin to plan my next steps from here. That's one massive thing I don't need to worry about. I look down at my cord knotted bracelet and immediately hear Lama's words: *Trust Sarah. To build your dream you must first let go of your resistance, what is ... is, you cannot change it. You must then focus on what you want and when your mission is one of true altruism you will attract all that you require.*

'Earth to Sarah.' Jane abruptly interrupts my thoughts.

I look up and as I do I feel a gentle peace flowing through me that lets me know that this is the right thing.

'Ok I'll stay. I'll pay you J ...,' I begin to say, but she quickly cuts me off.

'Don't even think about insulting me, Sarah, or I'll withdraw the offer quick smart. You will not pay me,' she says with a stern glare, but then smiles as she adds 'as long as you're okay with me popping in at all hours of the day and night with or without friends.'

She winked at me and got up to brew a fresh coffee.

'Hang on, you can't get away with that little comment,' I quickly follow her into the kitchen and sit at the breakfast bar. 'What was that about bringing a friend? You've got to tell me now, Jane.'

She smiled and looked like she wanted to say something but was still not sure.

'A-ha,' I knowingly say, 'Janie's got a boyfriend, Janie's got a boyfriend.'

I taunt her like a school-age girl and Jane's face noticeably changes ever so slightly from the big smile to something unreadable, something that almost seems to express disappointment and sadness. *Oh, crap* I think, *shut up Sarah and listen.* So, I do shut up and wait for Jane to speak next.

'I don't have a boyfriend, Sarah,' she says as she turns her back to make the coffee.

Oh God, what an idiot I've been. All this time and I've never known. Jane is married to her work I used to say, 'she' used to say—Why? —Surely that was an excuse while she was studying, but why has there never been a man in Jane's life, unless ...

'Jane, I'm so stupid! Why didn't you tell me?'

Jane turns back to look at me, and she appears somehow relieved, it's as though finally this heavy burden she has carried alone is out in the open.

'I couldn't tell anyone, Sarah. My family are Catholics, they could never accept the truth about me. You know how hard it's been for Uncle Sid trying to live in a world that would never accept him to the point that he has kept his secret his whole life. People think if the words aren't spoken then they can pretend it's not true or they can make excuses for the obvious. Uncle Sid is eccentric, or that's just Uncle Sid, he never wanted to get married, never had an interest in children. You've heard it all, Sarah, and you know Uncle Sid loves children. He would have been an amazing dad, and that's what makes this even sadder. The time just wasn't right for me to say anything, but the world is changing, people are changing and it's time for me to declare to the world who I am. I was born this way. It's not a choice, who would choose to be ostracised, excluded and ridiculed. Even worse than that, gays are hated and certainly not accepted in my area of work. Could you imagine how it would have affected my career if people knew? It was better to just keep it to myself, and part of me wasn't ready to even tell you. I just couldn't face disappointing you.'

'Disappointing me? You could never disappoint me, I love you. You're my best friend.'

'And, I didn't want that to change and believe me this changes people, it changes relationships. I was scared. I should have trusted in you, I'm sorry now that I didn't, it's been a lonely journey on my own.'

To hear my courageous friend declare that she had been *scared* struck me. How terrible it must have been for her. The person I always thought of as a trail blazer, always believed to be so strong, how sad for her to have to live in a world of judgement and hatred, but not just out there in the world, in her own home too. My respect for this woman continued to grow.

'What if you have underestimated your mum and dad, Jane?' I said really hoping that it could be true.

'You know them, Sarah, the church is their life. There have been moments when I thought I could tell them, but I never had the courage. I didn't want their scorn or disapproval. You know the Catholic church's view on such matters. Do good, be good, love thy neighbour, except, of course, if they are the same sex as you. I know it's rubbish, Sarah, I know my God loves me or He wouldn't have made me this way, but the fact remains, no matter what I have achieved in life, no matter what else I have done, all my family would see was the disappointment of a gay daughter. Why do you think I have strived so hard, achieved so much? I just wanted their acceptance, their approval, I wanted them to be so proud of me that nothing else mattered. I think of you and your mum and I feel jealous that I don't have that same relationship with my mum but I'm at peace with that now. I know now that their opinions are really nothing at all to do with me and everything to do with them. I can't change that, but it has taken quite a bit of counselling for me to be able to say that.'

Jane smiled, then said, 'I'm proud of who I am, personally and professionally and now I don't let anyone else's opinions hold me back from being me anymore. It's time for me now. If people don't like who I am, that is their choice. Their opinion is a product of their own life and their own experiences, nothing more nothing less. I will no longer hide or apologise for who I am.'

I walk around the kitchen island bench and embrace Jane and as I hold her, I feel so proud of her right at this moment.

'I love you Jane,' I say. 'I have always known you are amazing, but now I am even more proud of you. Thank you, for trusting me with this, Jane, I will stand with you if you choose to tell your parents and my family will never turn their backs on you.'

I take a step back and notice tears welling in her eyes.

'I feel so relieved that you know.'

'Me too. Oh, and don't forget, you can always borrow my mum any time you need to. You know she thinks of you like a daughter anyway.'

I thought about Mum and wondered if she already knew. I would not be surprised. She had a way of knowing things that were unspoken.

'So, come on, tell me who your friend is Jane?'

'You'll meet her soon enough, she wanted to give us some space. Her name is Kate. She's a psychologist,' Jane laughs.

'Just what I needed right?'

'No, seriously, Sarah, she's amazing, you'll love her.'

'I can't wait to meet her. I'm really happy for you, Jane.'

'Thanks, I can't tell you how important that is to hear, Sarah. Okay, enough about me. What about you?'

'Nothing to tell on that front.'

I feel a stirring within me as Matt immediately springs to mind. I ask her as casually as I can if she had seen him lately. My thoughts had not been far from him since I arrived home, particularly as we passed through Aspendale late last night.

'No, not since you left,' Jane sat quietly searching my face for hidden expressions.

'What?' I said.

'You tell *me* what.' She said back.

There was never any hiding anything from Jane, it was almost futile to attempt to do so, she could always read me.

'I think I may have made a terrible mistake, Jane.' I confess as I experience a wave of relief flow through me. There, I have finally said it out loud. Jane sits in silence and waits for me to speak.

'I still love him Jane.'

'I know he was really upset when you left, Sarah, why don't you call him. What's the worst that can happen?'

'He may tell me he hates me! He had to sell the house. He loved that place, *we* loved that place.'

Again, Jane just sits in silence.

'I've really hurt him. The damage may be irreversible. He may already have moved on. What if he has found someone else?'

She hands me her Motorola mobile phone and says, 'One way to find out.'

With that she stands to go outside.

I sit staring at the phone in my hand. I have no idea how to have the conversation I know I should. Again, I hear Lama's voice in my head: *Trust, Sarah, if it is meant to be it will be.* Was this meant to be? I wondered as I turned on the phone and dialled the number.

'Hello, Matthew speaking,' I heard the familiar voice and a wave of panic floods through me. I took a breath to calm myself.

'Hi, Matt.'

There was silence on the other end for the longest time and then he spoke.

'Sarah?'

'How have you been?'

'How do you think I have been, Sarah?' His voice sounded emotionless.

I couldn't stand to hear him speaking like that. I wondered if I should hang up and accept that some things once done could not be undone, but I had to try. I told him I was in Melbourne and that I wondered if we could meet and have a coffee somewhere. I told him that I knew I had no right to ask anything of him and that I understood if he didn't want to see me, but I wanted to speak with him if he wanted to.

He agreed to meet.

I knew of a nice café near the beach in Mornington and we agreed to meet there at the end of the week when he could get some time off work. I felt a sense of relief that I had made the call I knew I had to make, but there was also a nagging feeling of anxiety in my chest that was coming from a growing doubt in my mind. I didn't know if there was anything left to salvage from our shattered relationship.

I hung up the phone.

I closed my eyes and took a few deep breaths as I pushed those thoughts away. We had agreed to meet on Friday and that was four days away. Banyu would not be happy if I allowed my monkey mind to spoil the next four days worrying about something that is not happening now and may never happen. I said a silent thank you to him for his wisdom and opened my eyes to see Jane poking her head in the door looking at me.

'Big smile. Things must have gone well?' She questioned.

'Not sure. We are meeting on Friday in Mornington. Would I be able to borrow a car, maybe Kate's?'

'Sure, I'll ask her, but it won't be a problem. Better call our mum too, don't you think?'

Jane winked at me and shut the door once again retreating back out to the deck with her Australian Medical Journal in hand for some light reading. Jane had told me Kate's little Honda was parked in the garage permanently. She had been given a work car for some satellite work she was doing with discharged patients who lived in remote areas and she didn't have parking at her apartment for two cars. I glanced at my bracelet that Lama had gifted me as I once again noticed how things were just falling into place.

I'm not sure what had become of my own car. I left everything for Matt to sort out. It may have been sold and included in my settlement, I really didn't know. Friday I would find out.

I picked up the phone and called Mum. She was overjoyed that I was home and full of questions. I apologised for not letting her know I was back and told her I would come home to see her and Dad tomorrow and we could have a good catch up on everything then.

'We can come to you, luv. You probably don't have a car and we would love to see Jane and her new home.'

'Thanks, Mum, that would be great, and I know Jane would love to see you both as well. I think she has a car sorted for me for a few weeks, she's just checking. See you tomorrow. Oh, and Mum, I've missed you.'

'We have missed you too darling, you sound better, Sarah, glad you are okay. Can't wait to see you tomorrow. Love you.'

'Love you too, Mum.'

I hung up the phone and look out to Jane and give her the thumbs up. She nods and smiles a knowing smile and goes back to her journal. I pour us both a glass of water and go back out to the deck. Jane puts down the magazine and asks how it went.

'They are coming tomorrow, hope that's all right?' I ask already knowing the answer.

'Great, tell them to come to lunch, I'll stun them with my cooking prowess. I have a new BBQ and I know how to use it.'

Secretly we both knew with Dad around the only one to be using the new BBQ would be him. We both laughed. We didn't even need to say what we knew we were both thinking.

Mum and Dad arrived mid-morning and after hugs, tears, many questions, more tears and an extensive tour of the house, we settled in the lounge for coffee. It was great to see them, and it wasn't until I did, that I realised just how much I had missed them both.

While we chatted about my travels and plans, Jane got busy putting together a few salads and chopped up a breadstick. There wasn't much else to do but BBQ the meat when it came to lunch time, and as expected, Dad took up his position out on the deck tending the BBQ with a beer in one hand and the tongs in the other as he left the girls to do what he said girls do best, talk.

Mum wanted to know all about what I had planned. I told her about the retreat and how I hoped to help women like myself who were struggling with infertility. I told her about Banyu, Lama Ngawan and Raaj. We spoke about Melissa, and I told her how I was so proud of what she is doing over there and how she reminded me so much of her. I told her about all the things I had learned about the mind and the body and how a stressed mind leads to a stressed body, and how when I learned to calm my mind my body experienced a sense of health and wellbeing mentally and physically that I had not known for literally years, perhaps ever. I explained how I wanted to use this same principle to help people become pregnant.

'When women learn to calm the mind, the body can begin to function normally again. Of course, it can't work for everyone, but even if it can help half or even a quarter of infertile women it will be so wonderful. I know of the stress infertility wreaks on women, on families and on relationships better than anyone. How wonderful it will be to not only play a tiny part in helping create even one life that may otherwise not have existed, but just as importantly how valuable it will be to support couples on this journey; to give them tools to get through it and in doing so help save precious relationships like mine that would otherwise not survive. I wish I knew then what I know now. What a difference it would have made to me, to Matt, to the whole family. I feel like I have a lot of damage control to attend to, but I'm making a start and I know I am on the right path. I feel so passionate about this Mum.'

Mum's eyes were so encouraging and accepting.

'I was on Jane's internet last night looking at research on this topic and there was so much information about the benefits of mindfulness and meditation when trying to get pregnant, and not just for pregnancy, the benefits are amazing for health in general. I don't know why it's not being taught in schools.'

Mum had listened intently, she could obviously see my excitement. I continued on and told her what I also wanted to do was to spread a message. A message that I was told over and over again, a message I chose not to listen to but now I want to scream it from the rooftops to help others. I want people to know that they shouldn't wait so long. I want people to know that IVF is not always a safe bet as a backup plan. That's the bit I never knew. That's the bit I never understood. I just thought if things didn't work out there was always IVF. I want people to know, I need people to know sometimes IVF is not the answer.

'I'm sorry, Mum. I'm sorry I never listened to you. You knew all along that I was waiting too long, and you tried to tell me, but I wouldn't listen. I'm going to honour George in all this Mum. I'm going to make his little life stand for something.'

Mum stood up and came over and gave me a big hug.

'I'm so proud of you, Sarah. I know you will make this happen. It's needed, it's worthy and you will be honouring my grandson by doing it.'

We hugged again.

'Thanks Mum.'

I had never heard her speak of George as her grandson, and it felt nice.

Jane poured us all a glass of Chardonnay, I sat in the sunshine surrounded by my family and best friend listening to the sound of the waves crashing on the beach as I smelled the salty ocean air mixed with the enticing aromas from the BBQ and in that moment, I knew I was home.

CHAPTER 18
DARE TO DREAM

The next few days were a bit of a blur. The Melbourne rain had set in as it often does but I didn't mind at all. It had been a long time since I had experienced rain like this and there was a familiarity about it that was very comforting. The rainy days also allowed me time to do some research. I was getting rather good at Google searching and thanks to Jane's internet I was becoming well informed about just what was possible to search. I looked up anything I could on the benefits of meditation and mindfulness practices to reduce stress.

I stumbled across several names belonging to people already doing great work with "mindful based stress reduction" and "meditation". These were esteemed men of science and medicine, not your everyday hippies chanting flower power. These men of science had studied the benefits, they had published research and they were saying what I now also believed to be true. This was so exciting for me. I researched and read all I could on the subject. I was like a sponge soaking it all in. This was real, this was important, and this was going to make a difference to people. I also scanned the real estate sites for anything that would be suitable for my project. I really had no idea of exactly what I was looking for or where it would be, but I was getting a better idea of what was available out there. I was able to cover all of Gippsland from the comfort of Jane's office chair.

Gippsland seemed the obvious choice for me for my retreat. I may not have known the specific details of what was to be, but I certainly knew how I wanted it to feel. The same kind of feeling that you get when you travel to the beautiful beaches and unspoilt bushland of South Gippsland. The same feeling you get when you go to Wilson's Promontory and stand in awe of the beauty of nature surrounding you. Gippsland had it all from lakes to mountains, the choice was mine and now I just needed to figure out where.

There were a couple of properties that looked promising but first I would need to work out how I was going to make this possible. I picked up the phone and made an appointment to speak with the bank's loan manager for Thursday. I had $53,000 in my account from my settlement, surely that was a good place to start.

Uncle Sid contacted me, we had always had a special bond. He had heard I was back and wanted to take me out to lunch to hear all about my travels. He had once ventured to India and Nepal about ten years ago with a friend. It was an amazing adventure for him and I remember spending whole days looking at his photos and hearing his stories and I was so entranced by his colourful narrative that I couldn't stay away. It is always interesting to look back on such times and as I reminisce on those fond memories, it's funny to remember that as much as I enjoyed the curiosity of seeing the photos and hearing exotic stories, I clearly remember thinking at the time, no thanks, this is so not for me. I quite liked my western comforts and I was happy to keep it that way, how things change.

Thursday morning at 9:55am, I found myself standing at the bank's front door waiting for my appointment. I was dressed in my best "going to see the bank manager" dress, and I confess, I was feeling a little nervous. This was now so important to me I could not, would not, take no for an answer.

The year was now 1999, and although things had come a long way in the last twenty years, there was still a certain way women were treated by some financial institutions. Knowing this and being fairly "old school", Dad had offered to come with me, but this was something I needed to do on my own.

I entered the office of Peter Western, the Local Investment Loan Manager, and I instantly took a dislike to him. Something about this man made me feel ill at ease. Peter shook my hand, asked me to have a seat and immediately asked me if Mr Murphy would be joining us. Alarms began to ring in my mind as I said, no he would not. I then went on to explain that I was embarking on this venture on my own. I gave him a brief rundown of what it was I was hoping to do and told him that I had $53,000 to work with. He smiled condescendingly at me. We talked for a few minutes, but it quickly became apparent to me that due to the fact I had no current employment he was not going to even consider me. He said that he had to do what was in the bank's best interest. Perhaps if I came back with Mr Murphy we could discuss this further.

I protested saying that I naturally understood that I had no job "at the moment" because I had just come back from India. This was possibly not helping my cause because I noted another disapproving glance from him. I went on to declare that I could fix that in a week. I had never been unemployed in all my adult life. I have wonderful references and I could do relief teaching tomorrow if I wanted to *and* I have $53,000 in the bank.

Peter Western stood up saying as he did that he was very sorry, but the bank would consider me a liability. He extended his hand for me to shake as he attempted to usher me out of his office. I got up and turned to leave without a word. I was outraged.

Uncle Sid spotted me walking down the road from the bank. We had agreed to meet early so we could have a walk on the beach before we went out to lunch. He took one look at my face and knew that something was wrong. He embraced me in a loving hug.

'Great to see you, kiddo, you look gorgeous as usual now spill the beans, what's up?'

'Do you want to walk, Uncle Sid?'

The beach was across the road and it was my favourite place to clear my head and get a different perspective.

'Bloody prejudices,' I said. 'It infuriates me. Do you know the bank manager wouldn't even consider me without Matt by my side? He made the excuse that I was unemployed but didn't even want to hear that I could have a job tomorrow if I wanted. I felt it from the moment I walked in, it's because I am a woman I know it is.'

'I know a bit about prejudice, Sarah. I was a bit worried you may encounter this kind of archaic attitude when your mum told me what you were up to. Don't worry, we can work this out. I want you to tell me all about it and of course, I want to hear all about India,' he winked at me and smiled that 'Uncle Sid kind of smile' that made me feel that everything *was* going to be all right.

'Today is a good day. I've brought the Roller out for a run.'

He gestured across the road where I could see his two-tone black and grey 1953 Rolls-Royce shining brilliantly and deliberately parked over two car spaces so that no one would scratch or dint the beauty. I immediately felt privileged because I knew Uncle Sid's Silver Wraith only ever came out on special occasions. It was quite the spectacle and did not go unnoticed by anyone passing.

'You'll get a ticket doing that you know.' I said with a knowing smile, but I knew he didn't care about that as long as his 'love' was safe from damage.

'Can we go for a drive after lunch?' I asked.

'Absolutely,' he beamed.

So, we walked and talked a bit more until we both felt hungry. I spotted a café that looked nice, but Uncle Sid said, 'No cafe today, Sarah darling, I'm taking my favourite niece to lunch'.

There were several nice restaurants opposite the beach, and naturally Uncle Sid had booked the most expensive one. Our table was perfectly positioned to take in the beautiful water views; white linen napkins, expensive crystal glasses and polished silverware adorned the table.

We talked for what seemed like hours, over oysters Kilpatrick, garlic king prawns, smoked salmon, Atlantic salmon and a crisp bottle of local Sauvignon Blanc. I told him of my dreams and how it was so important to me to honour my experience in a positive way so that I could help others. We discussed India, the colour, the spices and aromas that make India so special. I spoke about my little friend Raaj, and how I was worried about him. I spoke of all the other beautiful characters that I had met along the way that had made such an impact on me.

After the longest monologue to which Uncle Sid patiently listened I finally said, 'I get it now, I didn't understand it before, but I get it now. I understand how it gets into your blood so that nothing is ever the same again.'

Uncle Sid just smiled and nodded, it was as though he was caught up in his own fond memories from all those years ago. I wasn't sure, but I thought I sensed a tinge of sadness, but I couldn't think why. Uncle Sid loved India. After lunch we went for a short drive around the Peninsula in the Roller. All eyes were on us as we cruised about. It was kind of nice and I so wished that Peter Western could see me now. As we drove we looked at the local scenery and Uncle Sid asked me what kind of property it was that I was specifically looking for.

I said I really wasn't sure, but it had to be functional. It had to be set on a few acres in a tranquil setting. It needed to have the ability to accommodate people and it had to have an area to gather and to meditate. I really wasn't sure exactly, but I knew I would know when I saw it.

'Fantastic,' he said, as the Roller turned a last corner back to Kate's car.

'What are you up to Tuesday of next week?' He asked through the open window as I closed the door behind me. 'I may just know of the place you have been looking for.'

'*What?*' I excitedly say but then reality struck me like a rock. 'But the bank,' I replied somewhat deflated.

'Forget the bank. See you on Tuesday.'

I heard Uncle Sid's reply as the Roller pulled away and it left me wondering just what he was up to. Right now, I needed to get back to see Jane. I had so much to tell her about my day and I wanted to get it all in before Kate arrived after work. I hadn't met Kate and I didn't want to be monopolising the conversation about my day when she arrived.

Kate walked through the door at seven and I instantly liked her. There was something calm and comfortable about her. A certain aura that allowed you to feel like you already knew her. I went to shake her hand, but she immediately put out her arms and gave me a welcoming hug. 'I've heard so much about you Sarah, I am so glad we finally get to meet'. She passed Jane a sideways glance that said *it's about time*.

We hit it off. As we talked throughout the evening she seemed excited about what I was proposing to do with the retreat. She just seemed to understand what I was trying to achieve. She regularly practised meditation herself and needed no encouragement to understand the benefits of such practices and just what was possible for the body when mind and body were working together in perfect harmony. 'I'm with you', she agreed. 'It's about time someone picked this up and ran with it. How can we help? I know yoga,' she added modestly. In fact, she used to be a yoga instructor and *she* was telling *me* how beneficial meditation and yoga can be when trying to improve fertility. She seemed so excited about my venture, I couldn't help but think of more of Lama's words: *when your mission is one of altruism, you will attract all that you require.* I had only been back a few days and already things were coming together. Kate would be a wonderful resource.

The rest of the evening passed quickly as we got to know each other better. Jane said that she may go back with Kate tomorrow if that was okay with me. She had to work on the weekend and would need to stay in town, but I think she was actually wanting to give me some space. I was meeting Matt tomorrow for lunch and I believe that she was silently hoping that I would be needing some privacy. I, on the other hand, was not so sure. I felt an anxious feeling in my heart once again at the thought of Matt, but quickly chose to push it away and enjoy the rest of my evening.

Mid Friday morning I parked my car and decided to take a stroll along the Mornington Pier. I arrived early. I wasn't due to meet Matt for another hour, but I wanted to take the opportunity to sit for a while. The water relaxed me and allowed my head to clear. I had meditated early this morning to calm the feeling of anxiety that persistently tried to take over whenever I thought about seeing Matt. It was strange to notice these emotions in connection with this man whom I had shared my life and dreams with. Never before had I been anxious to see him, but so much had changed in the last year and now I was not really sure of what reception I would get from him. I pushed these thoughts out of my head as I walked to the end of the pier.

The rain had finally stopped after two solid days and the skies were clear. The smell of salt and seaweed was strong in the air today and the fishermen had taken up their usual positions against the railing. I noticed a lonely catamaran bobbing gently in the calm waters, its stately mast gently swaying back and forth mesmerising me. I decided to sit for a while to breathe in the calm and tranquillity around me. I thought about how grateful I was for the beauty surrounding me and how blessed I was to be able to really appreciate it. People walked passed me chatting or listening to radios and talking on mobile phones, I wondered if any of them were really here, on the pier, seeing what I was seeing.

It was so long since I had been here, but it hadn't changed. For me there was a familiarity about the bay that was so comforting whether I was in Aspendale, Mornington or Sorrento it didn't matter. It seemed to ignite something within me as it extinguished something else. I closed my eyes and drew in my breath observing all I could see. I smelt the salt in the air and I could taste it on my lips. As I released my breath I allowed my shoulders to drop and relaxed into the moment with the warm gentle breeze brushing my skin and messing my hair. *Bliss* I thought, as my tranquillity was interrupted by the shrill sound of a fisherman's radio. I allowed myself to refocus my attention on the gentle lapping of the water against the pier. It's interesting when in a state of pure presence, you are aware of everything and also not aware. You can choose what to tune into and what to tune out from; this had been my saving grace throughout the past months such that I had become very skilled at the practice.

I was aware that someone had sat on the seat beside me, but I was undisturbed by them. The Sarah of old would have been embarrassed to be caught with eyes closed mindfully sitting like this, after all what would people think, but that was then, and this was now. I was a different person now. I was more at peace with myself and I was a better person for it. It really didn't bother me what people thought. My pain and experience had allowed me to reprioritise what was important, and what was no longer important.

I sat for another ten minutes feeling the most wonderful sense of calm and wellbeing flowing through every cell in my body. I was no longer anxious, today would bring whatever it brings. My anxiety would not change a thing and so why spoil this precious moment worrying about what may or may not happen. As I sat I sensed the energy of this person sitting next to me and I was aware that they too had chosen to stay, who knows perhaps they were also taking a mindful moment.

I opened my eyes and stared out to the water. It's interesting how even the light and colour of things looks so acute and different after meditation. The sea had taken on new vibrant blue and aqua tones and the sun was sending sparkles of light across the water.

I sat for another moment before I looked at my watch and noticed that it was now midday. I turned to look at the person beside me and discovered to my complete astonishment that it was Matt. A silent moment passed as we looked at each other before he finally spoke first.

'You look well,' he said tentatively.

'You look well too,' I said but he actually looked really tired. It seems that the last months had really taken their toll on him physically and emotionally.

'How did you know I'd be here?' I asked.

He just smiled and gently said, 'Because I know you Sarah.'

It was true, this man that knew me so well came early too because he knew that I would be sitting somewhere by the water. The pier was an obvious place to start looking.

We asked each other how we had each been as we made small talk. I asked about the business and how it was going. I avoided asking where he was living, it was still too raw. I didn't even know if he was seeing someone. I hoped and prayed that he wasn't but who knew. It was me, after all, who left. I am the one who refused contact. I am the one that made all the choices for all the wrong reasons. I didn't ask him if he was seeing someone or if he still loved me, if there was anything left he would be insulted that I could think such a thing. If he hated me he would think it was none of my business, and so I avoided the topic.

I would have to just speak from my heart. Tell him how I felt and hope that somewhere deep under his pain and hurt he still felt the same, but not yet. We walked on the beach and talked some more. I asked about his parents and how they were and told him I had caught up with Mum and Dad on Tuesday. I told him I was staying at Jane's beach house in Rye until I got settled.

I wanted to tell him about the retreat and India, but I needed to know first if there was any hope for us. These thoughts, these questions were now firing at my consciousness like a Gatling gun. When I saw his blue eyes staring back at me, I could wait no longer. I felt weak at the knees as the strongest feelings of love that I had suppressed for so long washed over me and through me to my very core. It was as though we were connected in some synergistic way that overpowered me when we came together such that the strength of my love was magnified simply by his presence. My futile attempts to deny this love were now melting away, like ice on a hot summer's day, leaving no trace of their existence. All I felt for my husband in this moment was pure love. How could I have pushed this man away? What damage have I done to him? I could no longer contain myself.

I reached out and took his hand and said, 'I am so sorry, Matt.'

Tears began to well in my eyes as I saw a spark of hope ignite in his.

'I have made a terrible mistake and I don't expect you to just forgive me or take me back, but I need to say that I love you more than I have ever loved ...'

Matt did not wait for me to finish talking. He took me in his arms and kissed me.

His kiss said it all.

Through my tears I could only see a blur but there was a relief on his face as the stress and tension of the past year began to fade.

'I love you Sarah, I have always loved you. I never gave up hope. We are meant to be together, you and I, together with or without children.'

He hugged me again and we stood in that embrace for what seemed like hours neither of us wanting to let go first. Matt moved away tenderly kissing my head and wrapped his arm around me, holding me close as we walked back to the street. I asked him if he was hungry, but neither of us were thinking about food.

I suggested that we go back to Jane's house. I was eager to show it to him and I could make us something to eat when we felt hungry. He agreed and followed me for the thirty-minute drive to Rye. It was a long thirty minutes. I needed to feel him close to me again to reassure me that this was real. Too much time had passed when we were apart and now I never wanted to be away from his side again. So strange how perception can change so much, I remember thinking as I looked at the clock. I'm sure it didn't take this long when I drove down this morning.

I pulled up in Jane's drive and Matt was close behind. We walked into the house and I explained that Jane had left this morning to go back to her place in town. I didn't mention Kate, that was a story for another time. I started giving him the tour of the lower level. I showed him into my room and opened the balcony door and sucked in the sea air. 'Isn't it beautiful?' I asked, as I stared out, onto the deck. 'It really is', he said as he came up behind me wrapping me in a tender embrace and kissing my neck. I turned around and kissed him back. The passion of that moment overcame us both and we fell onto the bed and for the first time in many years we made love.

We stayed in bed all afternoon. We talked, we made love, we drifted in and out of slumber and then we did it all again. I watched Matt as he slept by my side and my thoughts went back to the first time I had woken to find him asleep beside me. How much had changed since then, how naïve I had been about life and love. Matt opened his eyes almost as though he could feel the weight of my gaze and he smiled. A slight tinge of grey was apparent in his hair around his temples that had not been there before. It was obvious that we had both endured a lot.

When I finally looked at the time it was after six in the evening. 'You must be starving,' I said to Matt as I jumped up to get something to eat. He grabbed me by the arm and pulled me back into bed.

'Don't go.'

'I'm not going anywhere, except to the kitchen, come with me then,' I said laughing and throwing back the covers to expose his muscular tanned body as I turned to run upstairs. Matt chased me up the stairs into the living area catching me just as I reached the kitchen. Then he stopped and looked over the deck to the beach.

'This is absolutely stunning—Go Jane!'

We ate some smoked salmon and cheese that was in the fridge and drank a chilled bottle of Mornington Peninsula Sauvignon Blanc as we caught up on the last six months. I had so much to say that I didn't know where to start. I needed Matt to understand I was not the same Sarah that had left six months ago and that I couldn't go back to my old life, but first I wanted to hear what he had been up to.

Matt, in an attempt to keep busy and avoid falling headlong into his despair, really threw himself into the promoting of his business. He saw general practitioners and introduced himself and even did talks on the topic of health and wellbeing at some of the local schools and sporting clubs, with a focus on prevention rather than cure. These sessions had been very successful in getting his name out into the community and this, combined with a new website, seemed to have really paid off. His clientele had doubled, and it had been necessary after four months to take on two new part time staff members.

I was so pleased for him, work had always been important to Matt. It was part of his identity, how he saw himself in the world and he was very good at what he did. He said he was now able to take some time out when he needed to, just as he had done today because he had competent people to take hold of the reins when he was not there. This was a good thing because I was inwardly trying to piece together just how I was going to move into this next phase of my life with Matt now by my side. These extra staff would allow him some flexibility, which was great.

On Saturday, I felt comfortable enough to broach the subject of where he was living, and he teased me and said I would just have to wait to see. Later that day he came back to the topic and was some-what more serious. He said he wanted no secrets between us, so he wanted to show me his house on Monday. He had called someone from work on Saturday morning and managed to arrange another day off, but he would have to go in to work on Tuesday. He asked if I would come with him and stay at his place on Monday night, so he could show me around. I agreed.

We didn't want to talk about anything too contentious, so we simply enjoyed being in each other's company and in each other's arms. There was no need to leave the house. Jane had fully stocked the fridge, the pantry, and the wine rack for me and insisted that I partake in all the goodies, and for this weekend at least I was happy to do just that. I would make it up to her and restock when I left but for now, we were both happy to forget the world around us and stay right where we were.

I spoke all about India and how I felt like a different person now. I needed him to understand what I had experienced and why it was so pivotal for me. I needed him to understand how important it was for me to find the value in what we had both been through. How very important it was for me to give worth to George's life and my own. As I said these words to him, tears began to flow down my cheeks.

'He was here Matt … he was valuable, and he was our son and I want to validate his existence.'

Matt became noticeably emotional; his blue eyes were highlighted by the surrounding redness rapidly developing as he began to cry. The tears flowed. I sat with him and held him and let his emotion flow uninterrupted. After five minutes his sobbing slowed.

'Sarah, I haven't cried in nearly six months.'

'Cry if you need to cry. Let it out.'

With each painful sob his body gently rocked, his sorrow was almost palpable. He had been through so much. After a few more minutes he began to compose himself. As the tears continued to roll down his cheeks and mine, we sat in silence just holding each other.

When he was ready he spoke.

'I feel like a release valve has just opened and it feels like such a relief. I've carried this for so long not allowing myself to feel anything. I threw myself into my work, so I wouldn't have to think about any of it. To hear you say his name, to call him our son …'

We allowed the silence before Matt continued.

'I love you Sarah,' he finally said. 'What do you want to do?'

I told him that I want to help people, to teach them the things that I didn't know, the things that *we* didn't know. I want people to know that they can't always wait. I want to help people have the children they couldn't otherwise have and to help others just survive the journey. I want to help people's relationships survive this. I want people to know that even if it doesn't work out for them there is life after failed IVF and it can be so fulfilling.

I want to share my valuable lessons with others so that our George's life would stand for something. I want to dedicate my life's work to that little boy who never got to live in this world but who was so important and really mattered to us.

'Okay, where do we start?'

I talked to him about what I thought was possible, the things I had learnt in India and the latest research on the topic of meditation and mindfulness. I discussed what a difference it had made to me on every level, both mentally and physically. I think he could see how passionate I was about this mission. My enthusiasm showed as I beamed with excitement when I spoke about Banyu and Lama and the many lessons I had learnt. I told him that I truly believed that this is what I was meant to do.

I had a vision and God was providing me with everything I needed to make this vision a reality. I didn't have all the pieces of the puzzle yet, but the bigger picture was beginning to come into view with every day that passed.

I told Matt how Uncle Sid was taking me to see a property on Tuesday,

I didn't know much about it, but it sounded intriguing. I sat and smiled as I thought of everything that had already fallen into place since I had been back and then my smile faded slightly as I thought of my latest encounter with Peter Western. I told Matt all about it and how this man had completely disregarded me from the moment he realised there would not be a Mr Murphy joining us and how infuriated I was about it.

Knowing how strongly I felt about women's rights Matt laughed and said, 'This Peter Western fellow must be either very brave or very stupid to take you on, Sarah Murphy.'

'I won't let those archaic attitudes stop me, Matt.' I said defiantly.

I hoped he somehow understood that this was something I really had to do. Matt smiled and said that he would never stop me, even if that were possible, which we both knew it was not.

We enjoyed the rest of the weekend together and Monday came around all too quickly. I sent a message to Jane to let her know what was happening and that I would be gone for a few days. I parked Kate's car carefully back into the garage. Matt was going to drive me back. He said *my* car had been waiting patiently for me at his place; it had not been sold. I was grateful, another piece of the puzzle had just fitted into position. I had my wheels and there was no need to waste money on getting another car. *Yay! Thank you Matt, that's one less expense.*

We set off to Matt's place around midday, but he wanted to take me out to lunch at our old 'favourite place' first. We entered Vista Della Baia, our little Italian restaurant, via the side door. I noticed it hadn't changed at all. We were greeted by Roberto, the owner, who knew us well and immediately enquired where we had been for so long. He seated us at our favourite table and from there, through the expansive glass window that stretched the length of the building, you could see right across the bay.

I was reminded of the many evenings that we had spent sitting at this very table accompanied by nature's amazing light show of orange, red and yellow hues as the sun gradually set over the water. The twinkling of lights that followed was equally spectacular as day gradually turned into night and one by one the lights surrounding the bayside suburbs began to sparkle like little jewels.

It had been a long time since I had tasted Italian food and Vista Della Baia did not disappoint. We sat enjoying each other's company and it felt as though the last year was just a bad dream. We were once again just Matt and Sarah, and there was something so comfortable about that. I looked into Matt's piercing blue eyes across the table from me, those same eyes that for the last year I had avoided looking at, and in that moment, I was in awe of just how much I loved him, and how near I had come to losing him. I was determined that would never happen again.

After lunch we drove to the street of our marital home. I felt a firm tug on my heart strings as the street reminded me of all I had lost. This home I had loved so much, the home where our dreams were born, I wasn't ready to see it. I didn't know why Matt was taking me to look at the house, but I knew the thought of someone else living there was still something I didn't want to think about.

'I'm not sure I want to see it, Matt,' I said as he pulled up outside what was once our forever home.

It looked the same, and I was filled with regret that I had allowed this to happen to us. I scanned the front of the house from the driveway across our verandah and through the garden. I was just about to ask if we could leave, when I did a double-take. I swung my head back to look at the car parked in the drive.

'Matt, is that my car?' I asked confused. 'Why? How? What's going on? Why is my car there?'

I wasn't making much sense, I knew the house had been sold. I had the money in my account, but why was my car in the drive? I looked at Matt for an explanation.

'I couldn't do it, Sarah,' he said softly. 'I didn't sell it, I refinanced it. It's still ours.'

'Are you joking?' I finally managed to get out, but I could clearly see he wasn't joking. The shock of it took my breath away. 'I can't believe it. I'm so happy it's still yours, Matt.'

'It's ours, Sarah. It was always ours and now it always will be.'

He took my hand and looked tenderly into my eyes, I thought he was going to kiss me, but instead he said with a cheeky grin and a wink, that it was one of my friend Peter Weston's mates who gave him the money to do it. Then as though adding salt to my raw wound he added that it was probably because he was a *man*.

I withdrew my hand and gave him a playful shove. How could I be annoyed at him? But the sad part of it all was that although Matt was playing with me, he was probably right.

I put Peter Weston out of my mind and walked into the comfort of our little Californian Bungalow by the sea. I never dreamed that I would be walking through this door again but how blessed I felt in that moment to be doing just that.

At last, I was home.

CHAPTER 19
THE RETREAT

U ncle Sid was picking me up from Aspendale on Tuesday
morning at eight. 'Be ready early Kiddo, we've a long drive
ahead of us', he'd said. Matt had gone into work and I had already
been up and done an hour of meditation. As I replayed Uncle Sid's
words I had to smile, *this isn't early* I thought. My mind went
straight back to the five a.m. morning bell at the orphanage that
reminded the children it was time to get washed up and ready for
5:30 meditation and morning exercise at six. *No, this was not early.*
I smiled to myself, this was morning tea time.

I still didn't know where we were going. I was just along for the
ride today but part of me was very intrigued as to what the day
would bring forth.

Uncle Sid's beloved Roller did not get a run today. He arrived
instead in his brand-new S-type Jaguar complete with sunroof and
beige leather interior, right on time. Uncle Sid did love his cars. I
quickly grabbed my bag and we set off.

'Where are we going?'

In true Uncle Sid style, he said, 'You'll know when we get there.'

There was nothing else to do but sit back and enjoy the drive.

'How's Matt?' he asked as though the last six months hadn't happened.

I told him he was great, and we had sorted things out. He smiled and told me he was happy for me because Matt was too good a catch to toss back into the ocean. I had to agree. The sunroof was open, and the day was a pleasant 25 degrees. The houses soon seemed to disappear as we headed off along the freeway and according to the signs we were going in the direction of Warragul.

Up the road a way, we turned off the freeway and meandered along winding roads through a few quaint little townships and approximately one-hour-and-forty-five minutes after leaving Aspendale we arrived at the gates of a rather stately looking property. The elaborate and quite impressive wrought iron gates were locked with a large padlock attached to a heavy linked chain.

There were hedges surrounding the property that seemed to go on forever. When I asked Uncle Sid where we were, he raised his eyebrows in a "you'll just have to wait and see" kind of way without saying a word, as he opened his car door walked around the Jag and proceeded to unlock the gate. *A man of many surprises* I thought. I was very impressed. He got back in the car without a word and we proceeded up a winding driveway lined with an avenue of poplar trees in stunning autumn colour.

The lawns to one side contained many very established oak trees and liquidambars and some others that I couldn't pick. All were perfectly positioned to offer shade on the vast lawn area. The autumn colours were vibrant, and red, orange and yellow tones lit up the lawn. An ornate, wrought iron, centrally positioned rotunda offered further shade from the morning sun. I didn't know where or why we were here, but I was certainly getting curious. Surely this property belonged to someone who had a 'squillion'.

As the driveway meandered around we came to the top of a rise and right before us the main building burst into view. I wasn't expecting that. It took my breath away. It appeared to be quite old, but it looked very well maintained, someone had loved this building. It was made of red brick with what looked like concrete decorative work around the windows and roofline. It must have been about one hundred years old, built around the turn of the century. There was an additional building to the side that looked like it could have been a chapel and I wondered if this had been a school at one time.

As we pulled up outside the front of the building, I turned to Uncle Sid and said, 'This is stunning, but why are we here and why do you have the keys?'

'This property belonged to someone who was very special to me, Sarah. Someone I really wish you had met. His name was Michael and we were very good friends for thirty years. He was quite the whiz on the stock market and had been very successful as you can clearly see. He loved this place so much. We spent many happy days right over there in the rotunda with a bottle of wine watching the turn of the leaves just as they are now,' he said as he looked around reminiscing. 'How he loved this time of year,' he said with a growing sadness in his voice. 'Michael and I travelled together over the years, we went to India and Europe. He was lucky in life, but not so lucky with his health. He was plagued for years with one thing and another. Cancer finally took him away from me. He died, three years ago, after a long battle. He wasn't going quietly though, that's for sure. He never gave up. He tried to hide it from me initially until it became obvious, and I cared for him at the end right here. This place is special to me, it was special to us. He left it to me, I never wanted it, but he insisted. He had no family, just me.'

I took Uncle Sid by the hand and squeezed it gently.

'I'm sorry. I wish I could have met him.'

We sat for a while and then I asked if we could look inside, hoping that would lighten Uncle Sid's mood. He took a large keyring out of his jacket and unlocked the front door.

'This used to be an old convent,' he said as he walked me through the front doors and into a large foyer area. Two elegant stained-glass windows sat proudly either side of the door and shed a beautiful array of light onto the polished wooden floor.

'Michael bought it twenty five years ago after it had been vacant since the 60's. It was in quite a state of disrepair when he got it. He brought it back to life with love and his spectacular vision. He wanted it to be a country guest house at one stage and he refurbished the old nuns' quarters on the top level. There were twenty rooms up there initially. There's ten doubles now, all renovated. Nuns don't take up much space,' he said as he led me up the heavily carved original wooden stairway. 'There's a communal bathroom at that end where the original bathroom used to be. Michael naturally enlarged it massively and renovated it so that it now resembles somewhere that you would actually want to spend time,' he laughed.

At either side of the bathroom was a smaller private room containing an original cast iron claw-foot bath in immaculate condition. I had to admit, as someone who was quite partial to soaking in a bath, this place felt very inviting.

'He extended the plumbing so the rooms either side now had their own ensuite. Michael had impeccable taste, he spared no expense. This place was his love. Come on, let's look downstairs.'

Downstairs was equally spectacular. There was a large lounge area and a massive kitchen which had been big for its time to service the requirements of the convent. Michael had left it that way to cater for the needs of the guest house that was never to be. The truth was that Michael apparently just loved to renovate this beauty and of course, when he wasn't doing that he was apparently travelling the world with Uncle Sid. How curious, I thought, that this man I loved and thought I knew so well was living a secret life. There was a part of me that was not surprised, but another part of me that wondered just how I had not seen it.

We strolled through the lounge and turned away from the kitchen and laundry that lay beyond and proceeded down a long passage that seemed to run to what must have been half the length of the building. There were several small rooms which opened off the passageway, these were the original offices for the Mother Superior. There was one that housed a small library. I could imagine it would be a cosy place to sit and read and watch the flickering flames dance in the open fire place which was positioned on the far wall.

We wandered further along the hall all the way to the end and Uncle Sid opened the door with dramatic flair as only he could, exposing a huge room that looked like a grand dining hall. Highly polished wooden floors were the main feature in this empty room and the high windows specifically designed to bring in maximum light were made of beautiful stained glass. Uncle Sid was delighting in seeing the amazement on my face. He said that this used to be a multipur-pose area used for storage by the convent, but Michael had other plans. It was a mess when he started. There had been squatters in here for years so there was rubbish everywhere. He brought the timber floors back to life and never quite got around to doing anything else with it.

'Nice place to meditate, Sarah darling,' he said with a smile.

Yes, this is perfect but there is no way the bank will ever let me borrow enough for this.

'There's more,' he said. 'Follow me. I don't think you have been to church lately Ms Sarah. Let's fix that shall we, your parents will be so pleased.'

It was clear Uncle Sid was in his element. He was very much at home here and thoroughly enjoying himself it seemed. We walked outside, and Uncle Sid unlocked the doors to the chapel. The musty smell of an old building greeted us as we walked inside. This was the original chapel. It had been untouched for years. There was nothing I could say, it was stunning. Michael did not get to renovate it, or perhaps he didn't feel he should. Either way the old pews still lined either side of the chapel and the alter stood proudly at the front of the pulpit. I wondered how many sermons had been delivered from that very spot. There was an eerie sense of history here that made me feel pleased that this sacred space had not been disturbed.

'This is amazing.'

'It is indeed,' he smiled a knowing smile.

I dusted off a pew and sat down.

'Okay, so why are we here, Uncle Sid? I could never afford this place even though it was absolutely perfect and ready to move in and begin. The banks won't lend me anything right now, let alone enough for this kind of place.'

It was set on ten acres in beautiful gardens that provided the tranquil environment I was looking for. Even the location was perfect. An hour and forty-five from Aspendale. I could commute some days, stay here others. I calculated it would be two hours from Melbourne airport. It couldn't be any better, but I was beginning to realise just how much money I would need to buy a place like this. For the first time since I got home I began to doubt.

'Sarah, I think you know that you are very special to me. You are like the daughter I never had. You've always accepted me without judgement or question and your unwavering support has never gone unnoticed. It has got me through many dark days, I can assure you. I have been watching your journey from a distance, even when you were not aware I was there, ready to offer emotional support because that is all I could do. It broke my heart to see you going through such turmoil and pain. I had to stand by and watch the Sarah I know and love, gradually disappear into a shell of sadness and anger. But on Thursday for the first time in a very long time Sarah, you were back. My strong, determined, altruistic Sarah had returned.

You're so like your mother and I can see that this venture, this retreat is so important to you and it has reignited your spark. Your experience in India seems to somehow have brought you back from the brink and given you hope for a new future. Not the future you wanted or expected but life is sometimes like that. When you get to be as old as me you will understand that sometimes the most unlikely twists and turns can produce the most outstanding results. The twists and turns in both our lives have led us to this moment. What shall we do from here? You will need to be brave now and let go of your doubts. They will hold you back if you don't release them now. I know you can do this.'

'But how?' I ask.

'I want you to have this place.'

I could hardly believe my ears.

'And, before you say no, you couldn't possibly, I want you to know that I'm doing this for me not just you. You want to honour George with your work, to make his life stand for something so he will be remembered always, and you will do that. I want to help you do that so I too, can honour someone who was very important to me. A great man who was my best friend. A man who I chose to hide away from the world in life which I now sadly regret. I will not hide him away in death, Sarah. I want to honour Michael's life. He would be pleased to have his beloved home come to life again. It has sat empty long enough. When Michael died I just couldn't bring myself to come back. Too many memories, it was just too hard. I've paid gardeners to maintain the gardens. Michael loved them so much I could never allow them to become overgrown or die. I'm seventy now, what else am I going to do with this place? So, just say yes Sarah.'

I could not believe what I was hearing, this was too much to take in. I leaned over and hugged him, with tears streaming down my face.

'Yes!' I said.

This place was perfect. I was overjoyed, I felt a tingling sensation rush through my entire body and goose bumps on my arms. My head was spinning. My retreat *was* going to be a reality.

Uncle Sid brushed my cord knotted bracelet and said, 'I really like that kiddo, it reminds me of India and Michael.'

'Me too.' I replied as Lama's words came to mind. *How I wished I could tell him. So much had changed in a few short days, it was almost unbelievable.*

Uncle Sid interrupted my thoughts, 'Shall we eat?

It was after midday already. The time had flown by.

'I don't want to leave,' I said laughing.

'Who said anything about leaving? I brought a picnic,' he said.

Of course, he did.

He went to the boot of the Jag and pulled out an insulated picnic basket complete with bottle of chilled champagne in its own little Esky.

'Glasses,' he said as he handed me one. 'Let's celebrate!'

We sat on the lawn under a beautiful oak tree and ate cheese, salami, dips and antipasto and drank champagne.

'Here's to my little Great Nephew, George,' he said as he raised his glass to mine.

'Here's to Michael, a very special man who I wish I had met,' I said.

On Wednesday morning Uncle Sid went to the solicitors to work out the legalities but the bottom line was the title was to be placed in my name and the property would be mine.

It was now time to plan the next step.

CHAPTER 20

DHYAAN

The next six months were spent planning, researching and travelling back and forth from my new second home. Uncle Sid and I both came up with the name "Dhyaan Retreat" for the property. Dhyaan is Hindi for "meditation and care" and since the common link between us all and this project was India, meditation and a desire to honour others, we thought the name was perfect.

I had a vision and it was beginning, day by day to become a reality. I wanted this place to be a place of peace, tranquillity and relaxation. A place that was a refuge from the stresses of everyday life. A place that would lead people to understand that reducing life's stressors and anxieties could lead the body to begin functioning perfectly again in so many ways. I knew from my own experience just what a difference it had made to me physically and emotionally when I learned to be mindful and control my thoughts. Regular meditation practice had changed my world, but I was still learning more and more each day of just what was possible. I wanted to know the science of it and the more I researched the more I knew I was on the right path.

There were men and women of science who were saying the same things. Credentialed people; doctors, scientists, even professors of medicine who were indicating that the constant stress of infertility such as I had experienced would lead to increased levels of stress hormones such as cortisol that can interfere and even block ovulation.

I know with every ounce of my being that mindfulness and meditation allow a person to take control of the negative thoughts that would otherwise put that person directly in the middle of stress city with no means of getting out. All the *what ifs*, all the persistent negative thoughts, all the fears and anxieties keeping them rooted to the spot and directly creating a stressed state of mind and body which eventually leads them directly to the exact situation they were desperately trying to avoid.

I was learning more and more about the power of a person's thoughts to directly and immediately influence the physical body and my thirst for knowledge on this topic was insatiable. I had become very skilled at using the internet to source everything I needed. I discovered books written by doctors of Harvard Medical School on the power of belief over biology. It was so exciting I was like a sponge soaking it all in. I read studies on the placebo effect and just what was possible for the body when the mind believed something to be true. Research article after research article presented case studies on people who had responded in trials as though they had taken the trial drugs even though all they had taken was saline or glucose. The placebo effect was so well documented that surely this alone was an indicator of how the mind can powerfully affect the body.

Some studies indicated that people had complete remissions while on the placebo treatments but became unwell again and even died in some cases when it was disclosed that they were in the placebo group. It soon became so apparent to me that the body not only had to be given an optimal situation or environment from which to function at its best, but the other essential ingredient was the power that the person's beliefs played in achieving their outcomes.

I read stories about the Aboriginal culture in Australia and how the pointing the bone tradition would cause an otherwise healthy individual to literally die only days after having been cursed by someone pointing a bone at them. Surely this is the power of the mind over body at its best. If you truly believe you will die, you die.

I had seen the same thing with a mother at school who had lived her entire life in fear of getting cancer and sure enough she did. I also knew of a child at school who had such potential as a musician, who played piano like Mozart to near perfection, never missing a note. This same child, for some reason believed beyond a shadow of doubt that he would play the wrong notes at the grading competitions and embarrass himself. And of course, he did. He never failed to play the wrong notes at the competitions and he never failed to embarrass himself to the point that he eventually stopped trying. He said he wasn't particularly anxious about playing, he loved piano and just couldn't understand his bad luck.

I surmised if people could learn to use their natural ability to influence their outcomes to their advantage instead of their disadvantage, surely anything was possible.

Think about what you want, only what you want, Lama's words are again with me. Each day I was gaining more and more respect for this monk who knew so much about so many things. This monk who was the epitome of humility and who was responsible for starting me on this journey that was to be life changing for me and for others.

It seemed, as I researched further, the things that I required to successfully run this retreat were beginning to become apparent. As I researched further I began to realise there was another essential element to achieving a healthy mind and body and that was diet. Again, the Internet was alive with research and testimonials on what to eat, when and how. I steered clear of fad type advice and stuck to the researched evidence. It was clear that being excessively over or under weight would play a negative role in conception for both men and women but particularly women. The IVF clinics offered advice on diet and exercise and of course, smoking was a definite no-no.

During my research on mind-body medicine I came across many articles on the positive benefits of hypnosis to create positive change in thought patterns. Hypnosis apparently utilises positive visualisations and to me it seemed to be a very similar process to meditation, so I was interested to find out more. The clinical hypnotherapist assists people to challenge faulty belief systems and habits, at a deeper level than conscious awareness, and to connect to their resources to create change. Research evidence supporting the benefits of hypnosis seemed to be growing and it was clear that I also needed to learn more about this.

I wanted to do some more study to equip myself with more tools that would be valuable to me in my new role at the retreat. I had planned to teach meditation and mindfulness, but I wanted more. I enquired at the schools that taught hypnotherapy in Australia. It seems that there was every kind of course available, from a three-day course, which just did not feel right to me, to a diploma course that took eighteen months to two years to complete and also contained some counselling skills. Some of it was self-directed learning and done online and some was attended at intermittent week blocks of face-to-face sessions that would easily be able to fit in between the retreat requirements. I really liked what I was learning about this therapy and I decided it would be a perfect fit for the retreat.

I sent off my application and began studying.

Kate had expressed interest in the retreat and had offered her services as a yoga instructor and even as a visiting counselling psychologist when required. I had also sourced a local woman called Julia with extensive experience as a yoga instructor who was also a Reiki Master. She had offered to do the six in the morning yoga sessions every second day in the main hall and sessional Reiki. Jane, not to be left out, would also take up her position as our sessional resident medico. Her skills and knowledge as an obstetrician and gynaecologist would be invaluable and add to the credibility of our retreat. Uncle Sid would just be Uncle Sid. He had an open invitation to stay anytime and he would help out whenever and wherever he could. Matt would run the business side of things with me. He better than anyone understood the physical effects of infertility and stress on the body and he could offer exercise programs and even provide therapeutic massage if required. His business in Melbourne was now running itself and he felt he could easily divide his time between both.

I still needed to source a dietitian to structure healthy appropriate menu options, but this too could be done from suburban Melbourne. I had advertised and already sourced an excellent chef with great credentials who had run a retreat kitchen in Queensland, so he will be a great resource too.

Matt, Uncle Sid and I stayed up late many nights working on promotional brochures going over and over information and wording until it was just right and finally we were ready to go to print.

Uncle Sid had many surprising contacts and one volunteered his time to the cause to get our website up and running for a very reasonable price. This was great news to me as I could Google search with the best of them now, but I had no idea how to establish a professional website. Some things were best left to the professionals.

It was all falling into place and six months to the day from when I first journeyed to Dhyaan we were ready to open our doors to the public. I had advertised in the IVF support group's newsletters and placed leaflets in IVF doctors' rooms and the IVF clinics let me leave brochures in their waiting rooms. I thought that was as good a place to start and apparently it was because to my astonishment we were fully booked out for our opening.

Dhyaan retreat offered accommodation packages and stays that spanned between two days and two weeks. There were ongoing meditation and yoga sessions that were available to the public on a sessional basis and even day-trippers were catered for. The weekends were particularly busy, and it was clear by the already growing waiting lists that Dhyaan was filling a real need in the *infertile* community. All of our clientele was availed of the fresh organic produce from Dhyaan's onsite orchard and vegetable garden, lovingly tended by Uncle Sid's spectacular gardener. We also sourced produce from other local and regional selected organic food and beverage suppliers.

Private sessions of relationship counselling and personal counselling were available with a major focus on active listening and improved communication skills. We offered group support sessions which focused on challenging negative thoughts and taming the monkey mind. There were also private sessions of Reiki, massage, yoga and even dietary advice which were facilitated in the smaller group of rooms on the lower level that had lovingly been transformed into intimate therapy rooms. The larger gatherings were held in the main hall or, weather permitting, in the garden.

The chapel had once again been left in its original state, less the dust and musty odour of course. The woodwork of the polished floors and pews now returned to their former glory. Their natural raw beauty added a sense of reverence to this place that was befitting. The stained-glass windows had been carefully cleaned which allowed the light show from the afternoon sun to project its images across the chapel in magnificent style. The chapel now provided a space for Dhyaan's clientele to sit quietly and reflect in private.

As I stood back exactly twelve weeks after opening our doors I found it astounding to observe just what had been achieved in such a short space of time. There were people taking mindful walks in the gardens, a yoga class under the liquidambar and a meditation class in the hall. Private sessions were ongoing in the therapy rooms and the delightful aromas coming from Dhyaan's kitchen were wafting on the gentle breeze as the meals of the day were being prepared. This was what success looked like and this was what success felt like. I took a moment to reflect on the journey and couldn't contain my smile. The sunlight gently warming my skin, there was nowhere in the world I would rather have been in that moment.

Naturally there were teething issues, but I was open to hearing all of the feedback, so we could improve on any areas that the clientele thought needed improving, but the feedback that we sought from clientele was better than I could have ever expected. Just this morning I had received a call from one of our guests from the very first weekend who told me through tears of joy that after four years of trying she was finally pregnant. I couldn't have been happier. That was validation, that was success. It would be a long haul for her, but she intended to continue her meditation practice and all that she had learnt with us and she could not thank me enough. It was a strange but wonderful feeling. I was so pleased to have made a difference in someone's life, and this was just the beginning. This place had been my focus day and night for the last nine months and here it was. My vision had come to life but still I had an unsettled feeling inside me that told me I had forgotten something.

I commissioned a local Blacksmith to create some black cast metal name plaques for the various therapy rooms, one for the dining room, one for the main hall and one for the main entrance. He was also commissioned to create a series of plaques for the garden to be placed along the mindful walking path that had been created to stimulate the senses. The feel of the intentionally selected foliage and the aromas of the highly perfumed and brightly coloured flowers and shrubs, combined with the sounds of the pebbles crunching under foot and the rustling of selected grasses, made for a very sensual experience that was popular with the guests. It was always interesting for clients to notice just how much they usually *don't* notice when they are mindlessly rushing through life.

Rohan, our gardener, had already cemented the garden plaques into place where I had asked him to, and had hung the main sign beside the front gate. The new consulting room internal plaques on the therapy room doors were also now in position. The therapy rooms commemorated Lama, via a plaque announcing the Ngawan Room, Banyu via the Banyu Room and another one that read the Sid John-ston Room. These were displayed proudly on each door as all the staff members gathered in the dining area for the unveiling of the two remaining plaques. Uncle Sid and Mum and Dad had all arrived for the little celebration. Everyone had a glass of champagne in hand to commemorate the official opening, three months late, but nonetheless, and our chef had made a celebration cake, carrot and zucchini of course. I made a small speech thanking all those who had made this possible especially, Uncle Sid for his amazing generosity, and then I asked Matt to remove the cover to reveal the plaque beneath.

As the cover fell away it revealed the stately looking black plaque with white lettering that read The Michael Grifton Memorial Dining Hall. Uncle Sid nearly dropped his champagne. Tears of happiness welled in his eyes as he raised his glass and said, 'You will not be forgotten'. We all took a moment to drink to our benefactor, the wonderful man who had made this all possible.

With one remaining plaque to be unveiled we all moved to the main hall. Again, I asked Matt to unveil the plaque that hung above the door and as he did the black plaque with the white letters that came into view proudly announced that this was the George Murphy Memorial Hall. As I observed the plaque in position in that moment I knew that I had honoured the life of my son. I could not speak so I took Matt by the hand and squeezed it hard. I looked at Uncle Sid with eyes that said it all, and this wonderful man who knew me so well without further prompting again raised his glass and said, 'You will not be forgotten.'

CHAPTER 21
THE JOURNEY CONTINUES

So many seasons have passed since those early days. The beautiful trees marking each change of season with nature's brilliance. The budding of new spring growth leading to the vibrant greens of summer that oh, so quickly turn into the most spectacular show of colour heralding Autumn is upon us. This too, soon leading to more change as the barren naked branches declare winter is here again. The seasons that seem to change so quickly now are very noticeable here and are welcomed. I can't decide which is my favourite. It may just be the one I'm experiencing at the time. I find joy in them all. The library is my favourite place in winter. I often love to curl up with a good book and a steaming hot chocolate by the open fire in my comfortable pyjamas when my work day has ended.

Life here has been good to me. Matt and I still have our beloved beach home in Aspendale, but I admit we spend less and less time there now.

Today, as I walk through the garden in the early morning light noticing the frost on the grass which crunches under foot, I am grateful for my hat and scarf keeping me warm. I delight at the misty, crisp air that surrounds me as my warm breath becomes visible with every exhalation.

Dhyaan has matured and grown so much from those early months and over the ensuing ten years has matured and developed into something I could have only dreamed about.

As I stand in the early morning air reflecting on just how much has changed here, I take a moment to give thanks. Uncle Sid is eighty now and visits less frequently, but it is always wonderful to see him when he does come. I am forever grateful for his generosity without which this place would not exist.

I am sincerely grateful that life has been so wonderful to me. This is not the life I thought I would have, not the life I would have chosen, but life is sometimes like that and the most exceptional outcomes can often be the most unexpected ones.

Raaj was one of those unexpected surprises. He was more and more in my mind in that first year, so long ago now. I could never quite shake the feeling I felt as I saw his sad little face as I pulled out of sight that day I left the orphanage. Months later Melissa told me he had never been quite the same. He had his few possessions constantly packed in a little bag at the end of his bed for months after I left. He told her that I would come for him and he wanted to be ready. My heart broke when I heard this. It had been hard for me to leave him behind, but there was a part of me that did not want to uproot him from his country and all he knew.

The adoption process was a lengthy one, but he was right, eighteen months later I did come for him. Dhyaan is now his home and we are a family. He has grown into the most wonderful young man whom I am so very proud of. He eagerly participates in the day-to-day running of the retreat facilitating many of the meditation sessions and teaching anyone who will listen how to tame their monkey mind.

The sound of someone's footsteps interrupts my thoughts and almost as though he could read my mind, I turn to see my darling Raaj approaching.

'Morning,' I say as I put my arm out to greet him. I feel a surge of gratitude for this young man. We silently turn and walk together back inside.

The winter was turning into spring once again and Dhyaan was fast approaching its official tenth anniversary. The decision of what exactly we should do to celebrate this occasion was undecided.

I was in favour of having a small staff celebration, but the staff and Uncle Sid had other ideas. I bowed to the more popular opinion and continued to reserve my judgement.

Matt, Uncle Sid, Kate and Jane all thought that open invitations should be sent out via email to all past clientele of Dhyaan. The invitation would be worded in such a way as to invite anyone to our special ten-year celebration who believed that Dhyaan had changed their life in a positive way. It was to be an open invitation to couples and families to come and gather together in celebration. Everyone could bring their own picnic lunch and enjoy the beautiful gardens as they shared their stories of how Dhyaan had made a difference to their lives. Our amazing chef would bake some healthy treats to share especially for the occasion and frozen yoghurt and fresh frozen fruit ice-creams would be available for all.

I was a little unsure how many people would take the time out of their busy lives to come to such an event, but I again bowed to popular opinion and kept my reservations to myself. Matt, my wise husband, told me it was important to receive as well as give and that I may just be surprised.

The day finally arrived amidst much preparation, most of which I avoided. There was always plenty of things to do at Dhyaan to keep me busy and so I occupied myself with what had to be done and left the anniversary preparations to those most eager to be involved. Raaj was one of those most excited. He loved a celebration, and 'this was to be a great one', he said.

I had to wonder what it was that was stopping me from getting involved, was it that I didn't want to be disappointed? I knew in my heart what a difference Dhyaan had made to so many, but what if no one took the time out to come. Although, I was not in the habit of giving in to such negative thoughts, perhaps that was it. Dhyaan was my creation, it held such a special place in my heart, I did not want it devalued by a lack of interest. People are busy, and it is a big ask for them to come so far. *Okay,* I thought *enough is enough.* I packed away my negative thoughts choosing to recognise them for what they were, just negative thoughts, nothing more, nothing less. Nothing could change the fact that this place was special. This place had made a difference to so many. This I knew. I needed no further validation, but the ball was in the air and there would be no stopping it now.

I have to say the weather had been kind to us today. The sun was shining, and it was a beautiful twenty seven degrees out on the lawns. The trees in full spring leaf providing plentiful shade and the rotunda standing proud to offer even more. Raaj had placed seats about for people to relax on and he had decorated the front entrance and the rotunda with balloons and streamers. I hope enough people come to enjoy his hard work.

'It looks beautiful Raaj' I said as I surveyed the progress that morning. Guests were to arrive from midday onwards.

At 11:55 I peeked out the library window unobserved to see how things were going. Raaj was standing patiently near the driveway waiting for people to arrive, but they had not. My heart sank. I tapped on the window and waved to him gesturing that he was doing a great job, and then I went back to my office to immerse myself in my work.

At 1:15 Matt appeared at my office door.

'Come on Sarah, it really is time,' he said. 'You have to go out sooner or later and see who has come. It's you they want to see.'

'Okay,' I said finally to Matt. 'I'll be there in two minutes, just let me save my work.' Well, at least someone must have come, that's good. Raaj will be happy, I thought.

I saved what I was working on and reluctantly left my office and made my way to the front door. I reached out to open it and as I did it revealed a sight I was not expecting to see that stopped me in my tracks. I gasped at the sight before me as I surveyed the lawn area not quite believing my eyes. Dhyaan's lawns were quite literally filled with what appeared to be hundreds of couples and families who were all picnicking. There were children of all ages playing with balloons and chasing each other around. Raaj had gathered a group together and was running egg and spoon races. It was a joy to behold. Morris, our yoga instructor's partner, was playing acoustic guitar to the crowd and as I stood there, unnoticed for a while, I searched the crowd for familiar faces. I noticed Uncle Sid sitting in his favourite place in the rotunda accompanied by Mum and Dad. I had no idea they were coming. I noticed Kate and Jane on a picnic blanket on the lawn. I scanned the crowd almost in disbelief at the sheer number of people here and noticed many familiar faces dotted throughout. I recognised many of Dhyaan's clientele that were sitting and chatting to each other and at that moment my heart was so filled with happiness that I felt as though it could burst.

I continued standing on the vast front veranda of Dhyaan at the top of the stairs leading down to the garden, it was almost as though I was rooted to the spot. The view was spectacular, and I did not want to move.

It wasn't long before I was spotted by a man who I recognised from around eighteen months ago. He was sitting with a young woman who was cradling a newborn baby. He stood up and looked directly at me and began to clap. He was very soon joined by three more people, and then five more. Raaj turned around, Matt standing beside him and they both joined the applause. Very soon everyone was standing, clapping … me.

I felt the most enormous sense of love and gratitude flowing toward me in that moment as I looked at the smiling faces looking back at me; the couples I recognised that had once been on the brink of separation now standing hand in hand. The women holding babies who once never thought that was going to be possible. The happy families with children and toddlers running wildly around the lawns. It was only then that I was suddenly struck by the enormity of just what Dhyaan had achieved.

I was truly humbled.

The End

POST SCRIPT

Kintsugi, The Art of Precious Scars is a centuries old Japanese art form of repairing ceramics previously broken or damaged.
Each piece is tenderly repaired with lacquer and precious metal so that the resulting piece is stronger and more beautiful than the original.
Kintsugi teaches that things carelessly broken should not be thrown away but rather mended and displayed with pride.

My relationship with Matt, now mended and repaired with precious love, is different than before. Somehow stronger and more beautiful for the trauma we have both experienced, exactly like a beautiful Kintsugi bowl.

I am Sarah, and this has been my story, but this is by no means the end, in fact in many ways I feel it is just the beginning.

THE AUTHOR
DANIELLE AITKEN

ABOUT THE AUTHOR
WHY I WROTE SARAH'S STORY.

As a highly experienced nurse and midwife, I have spent over twenty years working at the cutting edge of IVF in Australia. Now a counsellor and clinical hypnotherapist, I run a successful private practice in rural Victoria, where I assist people to move through trauma and crisis by helping them to discover their inner strengths. When I'm not writing, I'm passionate about empowering people to achieve their goals and reach their true potential by working with the principles that are explored in the latter part of this book.

Sarah's Story, is a work of fiction based on the cumulative common experiences of countless numbers of women and men that I encountered over twenty years of working in the area of infertility. It's an inspirational narrative about self-discovery and transformation. A powerful story of love, life and resilience that leads the reader from innocence and naivety, through the emotional turmoil of unexpected despair and grief, then emerges out the other side as it skilfully illuminates human potential to triumph over adversity.

I too have endured my own adversities, as have every one of you, and I have learned from these adversities that although I may not always be able to control what is happening to me, I always have a choice as to what I think, feel and believe about my situation and where to focus my attention. For me, it was only when I realised that the illness I had been enduring, which had left me incapacitated on so many occasions and prevented me from functioning on any kind of normal level, was actually a gift that was providing me with an opportunity, that I decided to stop fighting what was happening in my own body and just go with the flow. It was only then that I discovered that this halt in the proceedings of my life had a purpose. This was my opportunity to stop, to give thanks and to write what needed to be written, and thus, Sarah's Story was born.

Working in the infertility industry, I experienced first-hand the devastation that infertility can wreak on individuals, couples, friends and extended family alike. It can often be an insidious and unrelenting issue and there are many relationships that do not survive the experience. I have utilised the insight and knowledge that I have gained on my own journey and sensitively displayed this throughout the pages of *Sarah's Story*.

I am blessed to be a mother of three beautiful children; Lachlan, Morgan, Rachel and stepmother to Jack. Grandmother to Imogen, Audrey and Brooklyn, I am currently excitedly awaiting the arrival of my fourth grandchild, and I never take this privilege for granted.

The purpose of writing this book was to shine a light of hope in the darkness that illuminates the possibility that sometimes amazing outcomes can be born out of the deepest despair and each and every experience can provide us with valuable wisdom from which to create a new beginning.

I hope you enjoy *Sarah's Story* as much as I enjoyed writing it.

ALSO BY

Danielle Aitken is an emerging Australian author of inspirational,
contemporary fiction novels.

Sarah's Story is Danielle's first book.

Her second book THE RIPPLES was published in 2020.

www.danielleaitkenauthor.com.au

facebook.com/daitkenSarahsStory

instagram.com/danielleaitken_author

www.ingramcontent.com/pod-product-compliance
Lightning Source LLC
Chambersburg PA
CBHW030639110726
47901CB00002B/502